"We agreed it wouldn't last forever."

"You told me that I brought out an adventurous side to you and… I'll admit that being someone else brought out something in me as well. But I always knew that the end would come, which was why I walked away and I meant to keep walking until…" he grimaced "…until I found that something inside me wouldn't let me carry on."

"You hurt me." Ella hated that admission but it was, even now and even in these circumstances, just too raw to keep to herself.

"I never meant to do that. Please believe me, but… I was born into responsibility. My family… I've been primed to take over vast business concerns. I could spend time explaining what that means in terms of my personal relationships but in essence, the life you want and deserve would never be one I could give you."

"I'm glad you said that."

"Come again?"

"I'm glad you said that because you'll know, from the start, that I don't want anything from you when I tell you that I'm pregnant."

Cathy Williams can remember reading Harlequin books as a teenager, and now that she is writing them, she remains an avid fan. For her, there is nothing like creating romantic stories and engaging plots, and each and every book is a new adventure. Cathy lives in London, and her three daughters—Charlotte, Olivia and Emma—have always been, and continue to be, the greatest inspirations in her life.

Books by Cathy Williams

Harlequin Presents

Hired by the Forbidden Italian
Bound by a Nine-Month Confession
A Week with the Forbidden Greek
The Housekeeper's Invitation to Italy
The Italian's Innocent Cinderella
Unveiled as the Italian's Bride
Bound by Her Baby Revelation
Emergency Engagement
Snowbound Then Pregnant
Her Boss's Proposition
Billionaire's Reunion Bargain

Secrets of Billionaires' Secretaries

A Wedding Negotiation with Her Boss
Royally Promoted

Visit the Author Profile page
at Harlequin.com for more titles.

HEIR FOR THE HOLIDAYS

CATHY WILLIAMS

PRESENTS

If you purchased this book without a cover you should be aware that this book is stolen property. It was reported as "unsold and destroyed" to the publisher, and neither the author nor the publisher has received any payment for this "stripped book."

MIX
Paper | Supporting responsible forestry
FSC® C021394

Harlequin® PRESENTS™

Recycling programs for this product may not exist in your area.

ISBN-13: 978-1-335-21334-1

Heir for the Holidays

Copyright © 2025 by Cathy Williams

All rights reserved. No part of this book may be used or reproduced in any manner whatsoever without written permission.

Without limiting the author's and publisher's exclusive rights, any unauthorized use of this publication to train generative artificial intelligence (AI) technologies is expressly prohibited.

This is a work of fiction. Names, characters, places and incidents are either the product of the author's imagination or are used fictitiously. Any resemblance to actual persons, living or dead, businesses, companies, events or locales is entirely coincidental.

For questions and comments about the quality of this book, please contact us at CustomerService@Harlequin.com.

TM and ® are trademarks of Harlequin Enterprises ULC.

 Harlequin Enterprises ULC
22 Adelaide St. West, 41st Floor
Toronto, Ontario M5H 4E3, Canada
www.Harlequin.com

HarperCollins Publishers
Macken House, 39/40 Mayor Street Upper,
Dublin 1, D01 C9W8, Ireland
www.HarperCollins.com

Printed in Lithuania

HEIR FOR THE HOLIDAYS

CHAPTER ONE

'COME IN!'

Ella looked at her watch. It wasn't yet nine, which was disappointing, because she'd hoped he would be late—very late. Late enough for her to tell him that, sadly, he would no longer qualify to shadow her, because the one thing Ella categorically refused to indulge was lack of punctuality.

This was not what she needed on a Monday morning, with summer drawing to an end and all the work involved in changing the store fronts, doing the end of season inventories and working out the various temporary placements that were needed to cover the Christmas season.

What Ella wanted was to have her routine down pat, as she always did. She liked routine. She liked order. She'd had her whole week planned out until she'd opened her email at eight, when she'd arrived at Hailey's, only to find that she'd been tasked with taking a lad under her wing to show him the ropes for the next fortnight. Jose Rivero, there through personal recommendation by Sir Ron Brisk-Hailey, whose family had owned the department store on the outskirts of Dublin for nearly eighty years.

There was scant information on why this lad was interested in learning the ropes of a department store but, reading between the lines of Vera's brief email, she'd concluded that he was probably a friend of one of Sir Ron's kids—maybe on the last leg of work experience before hitting university. It didn't matter. What mattered was that she wasn't in the best of moods when she heard that knock on the door.

Half-standing, reluctant, resigned and still resentful, Ella was smiling grimly as the office door was pushed open. She looked up slowly, schooling her expression so that she gave the message that she was a busy woman and wouldn't tolerate anyone who wasn't willing to do as told.

She froze as the guy strolled into her office, paused, looked at her in silence for a couple of seconds and then shut the door behind him with a little nudge of his foot.

She knew that she was gaping. She couldn't help herself. This was so *unlike* her, so *out of keeping* with her usual calm, competent, unflappable, *serious* self. There was part of her that almost couldn't believe she was standing here, staring at this man as though she'd never set eyes on a guy before.

He was...*beautiful*. Sinfully, crazily, stupidly beautiful. He was tall and swarthy, with dark, dark hair that curled just a little at the collar of his black polo-shirt, and had eyes that were designed to demolish common sense, reason and sound judgement—three things on which she prided herself having in abundance.

'I... I think you've got the wrong room.' She was irritated by the breathlessness of her voice, so she cleared her throat and did her utmost to drag her eyes away from the guy who was still looking at her with his head tilted to one side.

'Have I?'

'Yes,' Ella said sharply. She hurriedly tried to find Vera's email, leaning over the computer, all too conscious of those dark eyes on her. Then she frantically scanned it for details that weren't there in the first place...so why on earth had she thought that they would suddenly materialise out of thin air?

'You're Ella Campbell?'

Ella looked at the man who was now walking towards her.

'I'm sorry but I was expecting... I wasn't expecting someone...'

Was he going to help her out with this? Evidently not. His amused silence was unnerving, and Ella was seldom unnerved. A serious child who had become a serious adult, she had only ever been unnerved once, when her heart had let her down. But everything makes one stronger, and she had toughened up. So to be here, now, with her thoughts all over the place and her heart beating like a sledgehammer, wasn't what she wanted. Not at all.

'Please,' she said curtly, 'Sit.'

Ella watched as he sat. He moved with the economic, elegant grace of a panther. He was sleek, powerful and, sitting in front of her desk, he seemed to dominate the space around him.

'I'm afraid I just found out this morning that you were showing up, Mr... Rivero.' She glanced again at her email, blinking at her screen because it saved her from having to look at his darkly beautiful face. 'Vera didn't send over many details about you and, like I said, I wasn't expecting someone...' She sighed and linked her fingers together on her desk. 'I thought you would be younger.'

'My apologies for disappointing you.'

'I see here that you were recommended by Sir Ron?'

'I was.'

'I presumed that you were perhaps one of his daughter's friends over here to do a little work experience before starting university in Dublin.'

'I *am* here for work experience, but I won't be heading off to university, and I'm a little old to be mixing with Sir Ron's daughters and their friends.'

'How do you know Sir Ron?'

'Is that relevant, would you say?'

Ella met his mild smile with pursed lips because somehow his response, though valid enough, was just a little too over-confident for her liking—borderline *insolent*.

A young lad she could deal with, even a young lad who wanted to fool around more than learn the ropes. She'd had two shadow her in the eighteen months since she'd been working at Hailey's. But this guy...?

She was flustered. 'Maybe you could tell me a little about yourself—your work experience and what you hope to get from being here for two weeks. Do you have any experience in retail?'

Their eyes tangled, and for a couple of seconds there was silence as Rocco thought about what he was going to tell her and what he wasn't.

Jose Rivero. Jose Rivero was the owner of a small outlet somewhere in Spain who had pulled one or two strings with the owner of this once-prestigious, now down-on-its-luck department store, ostensibly to see how a big store was run.

Maybe his home was in London and he was hoping to open somewhere there. How had he pulled those strings? What sort of place was he hoping to open? The details didn't matter. He was just an ordinary guy who would be temporarily staying at a one-bed rented flat somewhere close by. An ordinary guy, a minnow who wanted to get in with the big boys, grateful to have cadged a favour. Smart, ambitious but with a long road ahead of him.

Earlier, when Rocco had sat having his espresso in the café opposite Hailey's, he had felt oddly free at the thought of his modest, unassuming alter ego. He would have two weeks roaming through the store, under the guise of seeing how things were done, while casting his eye over everything and making sure that he knew just what would have to be done to the place when he bought it to convert into offices and high-end apartments.

For the first time in his life, in the guise of Jose Rivero, Rocco would cease to be the only heir to the great Mancini fortune. He would cease to be the billionaire who had grown up in a mansion, who owned multiple properties, a super-yacht and a fleet of eye-wateringly expensive cars.

It felt good. It felt good to be sitting opposite this small, sexy girl with the straight dark, shoulder-length hair with the big green eyes and skin that was as pale as milk and dusted with freckles. It felt even better to be with a woman who wasn't interested in making a favourable impression on him.

Rocco smiled. He liked the way she blushed and tried

to hide it. She was in her twenties but trying hard to maintain the stern demeanour of someone older.

'Where to begin?' Rocco mused aloud, without any intention of telling her anything of significance. 'I'm just an ordinary guy who's been lucky enough to get some work experience here for a couple of weeks. To see how life in a big department store is lived.'

'You won't be seeing how life is *lived* here, Mr Rivero. You won't be getting involved in a set of a soap opera. The email I received doesn't specify a great deal but I'm presuming, from everything you've said, that you want to see how things are run?'

'Correct, but please, for the record, my friends call me Jose.'

'And please, for the record, I don't believe we're friends.'

'Perhaps not yet, but I've always maintained the importance of good working relationships in an office setting. So, let's start with my age. I'm thirty-two which, I gather from your reaction, wasn't what you expected.'

'The kids who come here are usually fresh out of school or earning money before they head off to university.'

'And how often are kids shown around the store?'

'I don't believe that's relevant, is it, Mr Rivero?'

'It could be if I plan on opening something more ambitious than I currently have.'

'Well, perhaps a handful a year. Summer time is popular and so is Christmas. We need the extra hands, and there are usually teenagers who want to earn a little money for the holidays.'

'Can I say that you look remarkably young to be in charge of running a department here? Because you are, aren't you?'

'I...'

'Not relevant. I know.' He held up his hands up in mock-surrender. 'Am I over-stepping my brief? I have a problem with that. So I've sometimes been told.'

'I... I'm twenty-eight.'

Ella licked her lips. The harder she tried to be composed, the faster she could feel this man getting to her, getting under her skin. He had walked through her office door, tall, dark and crazily *different*, bringing with him the enticing whiff of foreign shores and heady adventure. He'd reminded her of where she was—in a job she had never anticipated, living a life that had never been on her wish list.

A broken heart, her mother dying, her dad needing her...everything had fed all at once into bringing her here, back to Hailey's, where she had worked every summer as a teenager and then for several years between A-Levels and university.

Where were the years taking her? She liked what she did and she was good at it. But time was drifting by and her life was drifting by with it and now this man, showing up here...

She was only twenty-eight! Something about the way those dark, amused eyes rested on her made her feel conscious of her shortcomings. More than that, he made her conscious of her sexuality in a way she hadn't since she and Steve had crashed and burned. Since then, she had returned to the farm to help her dad and to process her own grief at the loss of her mother. That had happened shortly before she and Steve had broken up and put the sexual side of her into cold storage. The ice was beginning to melt just now and that was throwing her into a state of panicked confusion.

'Not,' she said in an over hearty voice, 'That my age has anything to do with…anything.'

'Of course not.'

'I…' She breathed deeply and wondered how possible it would be to dodge this job and hand him over to someone else. Vera had specified that she should show the man round because she knew so much about the store and because Pete, her boss, was off this week. But weren't rules meant to be broken? She'd never actually gone down that road but the thought of battling feelings that were suddenly at war inside her was a daunting prospect.

'I think you should fill me in on some basics if I'm going to assign you to the relevant department.'

'I would rather several relevant departments as opposed to just the one. The more I can see, the better.'

'Sadly, you don't get to decide where you go or don't go. Tell me what sort of shop you have and what areas are of interest to you.'

'A range of things, actually, although wine and everything to do with it is a large part of what I stock.'

'Really? Then why on earth would you want to look around a department store?'

'You stock food and wine?'

'Yes, of course, but that's a fraction of what we have in the store.'

'I would be interested in finding out what the profit margins are for that particular department in comparison to the others,' Rocco said smoothly. 'In a fast-moving age, it's good to find out what sells and what doesn't, wouldn't you agree?'

'Yes.' She was on more secure ground and relaxed. 'I think the white-goods department has suffered because of online shopping. It's so easy for people to flick through a website, find what they want and order it without having to trudge into a store to see what might not even be the full range of models on offer.'

'So true,' Rocco murmured.

She was preaching to the converted. He already knew the stats on which department was failing, and frankly not many in the store were succeeding, hence Ron finally agreeing to sell. Rocco had floated the idea two years previously. By then, his father had all but retired after suffering a stroke and, having been involved in his own extensive business concerns, Rocco had returned briefly to Spain to oversee certain changes he'd wanted to make for some time.

One had been to extend into eco-friendly, highly sustainable accommodation and office space. He had plans to be the leader in the field, and he'd met Hailey sufficiently often to have noted the decline in the department store which was in such a prime location close to Dublin city centre.

He'd made his move when he knew that the tipping point had been reached between holding on to the family legacy and letting it go because it was haemorrhaging money. He'd come here to make sure he wasn't being conned into paying over the odds and to work out floor plans.

He already knew everything else there was to know. In fact, as the woman stood up and beckoned him to follow so she could show him what he was actually not much interested in seeing, he realised that what he really wanted was to find out more about *her*.

'People can be lazy,' she said, walking ahead of him. 'Footfall in stores makes high streets thrive. Hailey's has been going for ever and it's the heart and soul of the community. The more people shop from home, the more a place like this loses its identity.'

'That's a very impassioned speech.' He caught up with her and fell into step. They had emerged into an open office space. Heads turned surreptitiously. She waved to a couple of people but didn't break pace.

'This is where all the paperwork gets done,' she said without looking at him, but bee-lining for the lift. 'Accounts, sales co-ordinators...customer services section.'

'And you're in charge of everyone on the floor?'

She pinged for the lift and he lounged against the wall and stared at her, noting the creep of colour into her cheeks.

'Not everyone.'

'But most.'

'I handle the sales team, customer services and oversee one or two other areas as well.'

'Tough call. For someone so young.'

The lift came. Ella stepped in, aware of him behind her and the way her whole body was burning, conscious of unvoiced questions surfacing for the first time since she had returned home. What was going to happen next in her life? What lay around the corner? She enjoyed what she did here, but was she really happy or was she simply biding time? Was this it?

She stared at the panel, mouth dry as uncomfortable thoughts ricocheted around her head. The silence dragged until she felt compelled to break it as the doors opened onto the floor below, dedicated to the failing section selling white goods, a handful of computers and phones, and the much bigger toy section which always pulled up profits.

'I've had a lot of experience here at the store so when I...when I had to return I was fast-tracked to a managerial position.'

'Had to return from where?'

'Had to return from the place called *none of your business*, Mr Rivero.'

Their eyes met, Ella's appalled at her lapse in professionalism, Rocco's openly curious at how her hackles had risen. That was definitely disproportionate to his inoffensive question.

Rocco was accustomed to women making themselves available to him and one of the ways they did that was to present themselves as an open book. They were always keen to elicit his interest. They didn't set about shutting him down by being abrupt. This was new for him. But then, he mused, he wasn't Rocco Mancini to her, was he? He was Jose Rivero and effectively she was in charge of him. She was going to be his boss for two weeks! He had to suppress a grin.

'Point taken.'

'Sorry. My apologies... I...'

'I see what you mean about footfall.' He adroitly changed the subject, because trying to encourage her to talk would have the opposite effect, and his curiosity was growing by the second. 'It's very quiet on this floor.'

'It'll pick up as Christmas gets closer.'

Ella frowned and saw the store dispassionately, through an outsider's eyes, while knowing what this outsider wouldn't know. Profits were down and had been for a number of years. The annual financial reports didn't make for pleasant reading, but the general manager was always optimistic. Hailey's had been a presence in the town for so long that they were all convinced it would never be allowed to fall by the wayside. It was more than just a store. It was the heart of the community. It was only September, but they were already making plans for Christmas and the traditional events they hosted over the festive season.

That said, there was no doubt that the store needed updating and that some departments were losing money hand over fist.

How much should she confide in a perfect stranger, though? Zero, she decided.

She pointed things out. She explained tricks they used to get footfall on the upper floors, which were always quieter. She was saying all the right, helpful things, while her mind was in freefall and her body responded to him in ways she didn't want.

She tightened her lips and fell silent as they toured the floor. She wondered whether she could palm Jose off on

Hal in the white goods department. If he wasn't around her, he wouldn't get under her skin and she wouldn't think about the parts of her life that were so unsatisfying when held up to scrutiny.

'We seem to be covering ground at break-neck speed,' Rocco murmured next to her.

'There's a lot to get through before I decide what I do with you.' Ella flushed at the unintended innuendo.

'Do with me as you will. You have my word that you'll find me a very able and enthusiastic worker. Your wish will be my command while I'm here.'

'Great. We love able and enthusiastic little worker bees here at Hailey's.'

Rocco burst out laughing, and he felt that something again as her green glance slid across to him and held his amused gaze for a couple of seconds. A couple of seconds longer than was strictly necessary, his highly attuned sexual antenna told him. Something stirred inside him, the thrill of being in a completely novel situation for the first time in his life, he thought.

'Maybe we could take a breather for five minutes while I process everything you've told me.'

'You should have been taking notes.'

'No need. I have an excellent memory.'

Ella gazed at him, out of her depth with this lazy banter. She wanted to escape this yet she wanted to bask in it and enjoy the excited, light-hearted feeling it gave her. Neither option was the efficient, brisk response she knew she should give him.

'How many more floors have we to look around?'

'Three,' she said crisply. 'And don't tell me that you're

exhausted. You don't look the sort who tires easily.' She cast a critical eye over him and reddened at the slow smile he shot her.

'What sort would you say I looked like?'

'Okay. The conference room is...' she nodded past the toy section to a bank of mahogany doors '...over there. If you like, we can recap on everything and then perhaps we could work out how best to put you to use?'

'Of course.'

He gave her a mock salute, which she ignored and walked towards the doors, stopping on the way to check out various displays that needed tweaking, aware of interested glances shot in their direction.

She would be composed and informative with him. She would work out where he could be placed—somewhere that wasn't in her immediate radius. In her own time, she would try and figure out why he had this effect on her and what it told her about herself.

Walking alongside her, Rocco had already taken in everything he needed regarding the state of the once-grand department store. He liked Ron, and had promised a fair deal, but it would be back to the drawing board on the price because he reckoned a full structural survey would reveal a lot more serious wear and tear than was on the surface. Probably more than Ron was aware of. He lived in Dubai and had left the running of the store to various board members—always a mistake.

She would normally have left the door to the conference room wide open. Stepping in behind her, Rocco half-closed it with his shoulder and then took the offered chair.

He was amused to note that she made sure to sit in one that was broader and slightly higher than his.

Trying to assert her authority? Understandable. But there was an electric current zapping between them, making her skittish and on edge. He hadn't banked on any of this, but he was enjoying it. He felt a little skittish and on edge himself. Freedom from the responsibilities that came with wealth and power was liberating.

Rocco's life had always been propelled on a very specific trajectory. His family might not be of royal blood but they were wealthy enough always to have mixed with the most elevated of Spanish society. Theirs was old, inherited wealth going back generations. One smallholding had grown over the decades and spawned tentacles that reached into every business concern imaginable.

As an only child, Rocco had been brought up to realise the importance of carrying on the family tradition. An empire needed a guiding hand and he'd had no choice in the matter. He was clever and ambitious enough to have thrived on the pressure. Had he ever wanted to break free? No. Not because he lacked the imagination for it but because he had an unerring contempt for where that path led.

His uncle, older than his father and the natural heir to the Mancini empire, had gone off the rails. In the process he'd come close to ruining not just the family fortune but all the livelihoods that depended on the jobs the Mancini empire supported. He had found drink, drugs and women too irresistible, and the wealth at his disposal had made acquiring all three far too easy for an inherently weak man. Maybe he could have ridden that tide until he got too old to maintain it or ran out of steam, but he had made the mistake of marrying one of his hangers-on— an avaricious woman in her forties who had fleeced him for so much money that she had almost brought the company to its knees.

After less than two years of a volatile and desperate marriage, she had hired a clever lawyer who had done his utmost to slice off various arms of the company as part of the settlement. His uncle had also signed over part of his own holdings to her at some point, presumably when he was high on drugs. It had been a mess.

It had also been a learning curve for a teenager who had watched from the sidelines and taken it all in. Control had become Rocco's byword. His parents' marriage might have started life as a business arrangement, but it had worked perfectly. There had been no room for misunderstandings. His mother, from a similar background, had known from the start what duty and responsibility looked like. She had been the perfect wife. She had known how to entertain the clients and how to be supportive without expecting any reward.

Rocco found that he was curious about Ella's life. He'd always mixed in a circle that was small and reflected his own life. Had he been lazy in that respect? Maybe. But Jose Rivero, as he now was, was seeing a side to life he didn't have much experience of, and it had whetted his appetite to see a little more.

And a little bit more of the woman sitting opposite him, looking at him with narrowed eyes and a professional coolness that couldn't quite conceal an awareness of him that was pleasingly titillating.

'So...' Rocco drawled.

'So?' Her eyebrows arched upwards. 'I think it might be a good idea to set you on some of the little jobs that might seem boring but are crucial to the successful running of a company.'

'Tell me more. I'm eager to learn.'

'Filing.'

'You want *me* to do the filing?' Rocco couldn't hide his honest reaction to that suggestion.

'Yes. There's a lot of it waiting to be done.'

'Surely you don't still use those antiquated things called *filing cabinets*?'

'We're gradually transferring everything online.'

'When did you start doing that?'

'There's no need to sound so incredulous. Hailey's is an old-fashioned store. Perhaps it could have moved more quickly in that respect but as soon as I got here, and saw how archaic the IT systems were, I looked into an upgrade...'

Rocco considered her for a few seconds in stretching silence until she reddened and began to fidget under his unwavering stare.

She really was incredibly pretty, he thought. Sexy in a way that wasn't obvious. Sexy without wanting to be sexy.

Why was she still single? Or was she? Curiosity was in charge. He wasn't sure he liked that, because he was so accustomed to his head ruling everything, but this was a moment in time that would never come back, so why not enjoy it? He settled lower into the chair, crossed his legs and loosely linked his fingers together on his stomach.

Ella thought he looked totally relaxed. He looked like

the guy calling the shots, which was ridiculous, because *she* was the one in charge here. She might not feel quite as in charge as she would have wished but she was still the boss.

But the way he was looking at her... Her mouth went dry, and for the life of her she couldn't drag disobedient eyes away from his face.

'So,' she said weakly. 'Back to the filing...'

'What did you study at university?'

'I beg your pardon?'

'I was just interested. Interested in knowing how you ended up working here, at this store. Did you study business? Accounting?'

'Geography,' Ella heard herself say abruptly.

'I guess that's a generic enough subject.'

Ella wanted to pull back from the conversation but something was urging her on. She hadn't much experience of this—of opening up, of straying out of her comfort zone... Her life had been on hold ever since she'd returned here. Maybe part of her life had always been on hold because she'd always played it safe.

She licked her lips and felt a slow fire inside her as those deep, dark eyes continued to look at her in silent appraisal.

'I didn't get the chance to finish my degree,' Ella confessed in a rushed undertone. 'I...my mother died. She'd been ill for a while—cancer. I was twelve at the time and I remember what that was like...but the cancer had gone into remission.'

'I'm sorry, Ella.'

The genuine sympathy in his voice opened up something inside her. Did she want that something to be opened up? Maybe not, but for the first time she wanted to confide.

'It returned in little baby steps,' she said, glancing down at her hands, which she then balled into fists. 'But then it seemed to snowball until she couldn't fight it any longer. When she died I came back here but…'

'But…?'

'But I guess this wasn't where my dreams lay.'

'Where did they lie, those dreams of yours?'

'I fancied getting involved in efforts to combat climate change.' Ella suddenly laughed. 'I was a big dreamer.'

'Sounds like a perfectly reasonable dream. But landing this job…it must have seemed like a stroke of luck. Like I've said, you're young to be in such a position of seniority.'

'I worked here over the holidays from the age of fourteen,' Ella confided. 'My mum worked in the haberdashery department and she pulled a few strings to get me temp jobs in the store so that I could have pocket money for the summer hols. After my Leaving Certificate, I came back and worked for a few years to save for my tuition fees at university. I didn't want to have a student loan outstanding.'

She cleared her throat and, when she yanked herself back to reality, she was appalled to consider how much she had revealed to a perfect stranger. Appalled and just a little bit…alarmed. What on earth was going on with her?

'Apologies. I went off-topic,' Ella said briskly. 'You're here for practical advice so, if you have any questions, please feel free to ask provided they pertain to the reason you're here.'

'Just the one.'

'What's that?'

'Can I shadow you for the duration of my stay here? I think I would learn a lot more with one dedicated mentor than if I flitted from department to department under the supervision of random people, picking up all the boring back-room jobs no one is interested in doing.'

'How do you know I won't lumber you with the same back-room jobs?'

'I don't, but I'm willing to take the chance.'

'I really can't promise that you can spend your time here under my sole supervision.' But her heart was thudding and she felt as though she needed to clear her head. Right now she wasn't in charge of her emotions. She was behaving unprofessionally and allowing him to get under her skin. If she didn't get some air, at the risk of appearing rude, then she was going to explode. No, worse—she was going to carry on waging war with common sense and that wouldn't do.

She thought of Steve and what he had put her through. She had been led astray by her emotions into ignoring red flags and handing her heart over to a guy who had never deserved it. Right now, the ground was shifting under her feet, and it was imperative that she didn't allow that to happen.

'Look at the time!' She stood up, leaving him no choice but to follow suit.

He stood up slowly and she followed that easy, graceful motion with fascinated attention.

He looked at his watch. 'Time flies when you're having fun,' he drawled and Ella felt that, yes, he couldn't have hit the nail on the head more accurately. She'd been having fun! It was crazy. She was supposed to give orders and do a job!

'I'm afraid I have some important chores to do in town but I'll hand you over to one of my colleagues at the staff canteen and you can grab some lunch there.'

'And when you get back…?'

'When I return, I'll settle you in front of some…'

'Filing. I can transpose everything onto the system.'

'Would you know how to do that?'

'I can confidently tell you that it won't be a problem. And if I have more questions…?'

'Naturally, that's what I'm here for.' Ella's eyes locked with his and her heart picked up pace.

'I'm glad to hear that. And would you be prepared to answer them over dinner with me…?'

CHAPTER TWO

Over dinner with me?

What a nerve! He was there to shadow her, follow her instructions! Basically, when she thought about it, she was *his boss* for two weeks. He was on a par with Claire and Sharon, the eighteen-year-olds who constantly had to be told off for giggling and trying on make-up when no customers were waiting to be served.

Admittedly, there were some differences… Jose was thirty-two, wouldn't know how to giggle if he took a course on it and was a drop-dead-gorgeous, sex-on-legs guy. But she was *still his boss for two weeks!* Which was why she'd given him a cool, amused, derisory look four days ago when he'd voiced that outrageous suggestion.

Nevertheless, she'd felt a tingle of awareness race through her at the thought of having dinner with him, of seeing him outside the confines of the store. And, over the following few days, she'd been aware of him in ways that were scary and thrilling at the same time. She would park him at a desk and point out what she wanted him to do but, instead of getting on with her own workload, she'd find herself sliding little glances across at him while her imagination ran riot.

When she showed him around the various departments, she was aware of how every single person in the entire store looked at him with interest and curiosity.

Ella knew he was dangerous. At least, dangerous *for her*. Temptation happened on a daily basis: a murmured remark, a raised eyebrow, a slow smile... Little ripples in her previously calm existence bit by bit were waking her up to a general dissatisfaction about her life which she had successfully managed to ignore since she'd returned to the family home.

The breath of *something more out there* that he had brought with him on day one didn't fade as the days went by. It got stronger, stirring a restlessness inside her she couldn't control.

She was beginning to find excuses to come in a bit earlier than usual and to leave a bit later. Was it her imagination or was he doing the same?

Ella glanced at her phone. It was Friday and it was five-thirty. She could have clocked off at five.

At the desk next to her, Jose was doing something diligent in front of the computer. He was proving to be surprisingly efficient at pretty much everything she threw at him.

'Ahem.' Ella cleared her throat and swivelled her chair so that she faced him.

Today he wore a pale-blue polo shirt and black jeans. Her eyes drifted to the bulge of his muscled forearms and the taut pull of the jeans over his thighs.

He turned his chair to face her and leaned back, arms folded behind his head. 'Ahem?'

'It's okay for you to leave now, Jose. It's Friday, and I'm sure you have lots of things planned.'

'Why would you assume that when I'm new to the area? Takes time to make friends.'

'You don't seem to be doing too badly on that front.'

'Have you been keeping tabs on me, by any chance?'

He grinned, and Ella reddened. 'Of course not!'

'It *is* your job, though, now that I mention it. You wouldn't want me to accidentally delete something.'

'That wouldn't happen. There are back-up systems in place. I'm surprised you don't know that.'

Was this the sort of Big Retail Store Experience Jose had envisaged when he had wrangled his fortnight here? He never revealed anything. At first, she had vaguely wondered what he was doing here, when everything about him suggested a guy who could take on what life had to offer without anyone's help, but she had shrugged away her curiosity. He'd come via Sir Ron and it wasn't up to her to start playing detective just because he didn't look the part.

'Anyway...' She stood up and shuffled stuff on her desk, tidying things away and very much aware of his dark eyes on her. 'I should get going.'

'Big plans for the weekend?'

Did the cinema with a girlfriend on a Saturday count as 'big plans'? Ella wondered. 'Huge.'

'Well, spare a thought for me.' Rocco stood up, taking his time, flexing his muscles and not ungluing his eyes from her face.

'Why would I do that?'

'I'll be on my own on my last weekend here, watching television and eating a boxed meal for one.'

'I'm sure you could rustle up some company from the fan base you've made at the store,' Ella said politely. She hovered, unsettled by what he had said about this weekend being his last one here, which was a reminder that this strange excitement that filled her whenever he was around came with a deadline.

She considered her life beyond him with a sinking feeling of dread. Her heartbeat quickened and she licked her lips and continued to hover.

Rocco felt the blood rushing through his veins as he held her indecisive stare with lazy, shuttered intensity. He fancied her. He had no idea why he did, when that had happened or how he had managed to surrender his self-control, because he'd never thought coming here on a fortnight's recce would include this scenario. He didn't like complications and he especially didn't like complications when they involved women.

Reality had no room for sentiment, and sentiment was the enemy of control—just look at his uncle. That said, this was a different place, far removed from the usual concerns he would have in a situation like this. Jose Rivero didn't have an uncle who had squandered millions and nearly brought the family name to ruin. Jose Rivero was free of those constraints.

Right now, Ella was hovering, waiting, for...what? Waiting for their conversation to continue?

Rocco felt the sharp excitement of adrenaline race through him. 'I feel I should apologise,' he said huskily and then held her gaze when she frowned with confusion.

'Okay, feel free. Go right ahead, although I have no idea what you want to apologise about. Unless,' she said, eyebrows raised, 'You've done something wrong on the system and were too ashamed to tell me? I get the feeling that you don't like being wrong but we all make mistakes.'

'Thank you for being so magnanimous and understanding,' Rocco said humbly. 'But I don't make mistakes when it comes to tech.'

'Oh, really.'

'Generally speaking, hand on heart, I don't tend to make many mistakes.'

'Can I say that that's a very arrogant statement?'

'Of course you can.' He'd been spot-on with the body language interpretation, he decided. It was Friday, and the weekend lay ahead, but she wanted to be right here in a deserted office chatting with him. Where were her *huge* plans—awaiting postponement?

Dinner would be very satisfactory for both of them.

'So, what do you want to apologise for?'

'For asking you out to dinner a few days ago when I first met you.'

'Ah. Well…'

'You must have found that very offensive.' He began gathering his bits and pieces, such as they were, not looking at her but aware of her with every nerve in his body.

Eventually, when he did look at her, she was blushing and still indecisively hovering in the same spot.

'I…' she began.

'You must have thought me incredibly full of myself, which—and I'll freely admit this—I have occasionally been accused of. Didn't you just do that—accuse me of arrogance when I thought I was just being honest? I'm always mystified by other people's assumptions.'

'Naturally, it seemed...uh...a little surprising. Dinner...'

Rocco strolled towards the lift and was gratified when she fell into step with him. 'For starters, I never even asked whether you were involved with someone...' He looked down at her, at the way her shiny dark hair dropped in a straight sheet to her shoulders, at the economical grace of her movements as she walked and the swell of her breasts pushing against the pale-blue shirt primly buttoned up to her neck.

She was so *different*, so *composed*, so *cool*, so *reserved*... He got a kick every morning when he came in to find her there, in her starchy outfits that did nothing to conceal her innate sexiness. Now, his libido kicked into painful gear as he continued to stare at her. They hit the lift button and when the doors opened he stepped aside so that she could brush past him.

'Are you?' he asked, leaning against the mirrored wall and gazing at her with interest. 'Involved with someone?'

'That's none of your business.'

'It is, because I would really like to have dinner with you, but obviously if you have a partner then I'll back off. I've never been the sort of guy who treads on another man's toes. So, are you involved with someone? Because if not then I'd like to take you out to dinner.'

'Why?'

'Sorry?' Rocco was momentarily taken aback. He stepped out onto the ground floor and allowed her to precede him.

Here there were signs of life, although with only fifteen minutes till closing, there was the depressing atmosphere of the few customers there politely being ushered towards the exit. Half the staff appeared to have vanished, probably getting ready to join the Friday evening stampede out. Canned music added to the general air of a place just waiting for the axe to fall. He could have left after day one from what he'd seen, but he'd stayed put. He was beginning to see why.

'Why,' she repeated as they left the store, 'Do you want to take me out to dinner?'

'Because.'

'You're going to be here for another week. Like you said, this is your last weekend, so it's not because you want to get to know me better.'

'You wanted to continue studying geography. You wanted a part in changing the world. You're serious about climate change. But you ended up here because your mother died and…was there no one else to save the day? What's wrong with wanting to find out a bit more about someone? So, tell me, was it all on your shoulders?'

'I didn't *save the day*. I came to help my dad out. He has a small farm. He needed someone to be there for him. He was…he wasn't functioning. Couldn't function. He was too wrapped up in grief.'

'What about siblings?'

'Honestly, I have no idea how we've drifted to this!'

'Because, like I said, I want to get to know you better. You aren't only interested in someone if they're going to become a permanent fixture in your life. Aside from all of that, I find you attractive.'

'Really.' Her voice was thick with scepticism.

'Yes, really. Tell me where this is coming from. You're very, very sexy—has no one ever told you that before?' He raised his eyebrows at her expression. 'Why are you looking at me with such a scathing expression? Doesn't make you any less sexy, if you want to know. We can explore that later. First, answer my question. Is there someone in your life? My gut tells me no, but only a fool obeys his gut.'

'No,' Ella said impatiently, 'I'm not involved with anyone.'

'Then have dinner with me. I know a good restaurant. I walk past it on my way to…where I'm renting. Nice atmosphere, always busy. Menu looks good…'

Ella could feel her heart thudding like a sledgehammer as she stared up at him.

It was busy outside the store. Everyone was out enjoying the dregs of summer before autumn and winter blew in, with jolly Christmas songs and cheerful reminders of what she was missing on the man front. The coffee shop opposite thronged with customers.

He found her attractive. He thought she was sexy. She should be wary of that, should have her guard up. Trusting a man wasn't on her radar.

And yet…and yet… Here she was, guard up, being careful, settling into a life where nothing exciting ever happened because she'd been hurt, because she was cautious. And here was this man, a stranger who would leave her life for ever in a week… A stranger who had made her look at her own life and see what it lacked.

Ella was suddenly filled with a sense of reckless adventure, a feeling that life was slipping past her and, if she didn't reach out to catch it, then by the time she woke up it might be too late.

'Okay. Yes.' She smiled hesitantly as their eyes tangled.

'Good.' Rocco drawled. 'Because I want to know all about Ella and why she was so surprised when I told her that I found her attractive.'

He began strolling away from the store and she kept pace. She knew where this was going and she wanted it to go there. She wanted to break out of the walls she had built around herself and see what a bit of adventure tasted like. It was almost too exciting to think about.

There was freedom in knowing he wouldn't be sticking around. She could do what she wanted, say what she wanted, they could have a good time for the next week and then he would be gone for ever. She was walking on air, barely aware of being shown to a table in the buzzy wine bar or wine being ordered.

'Talk to me, Ella,' he purred as soon as wine had been poured for them. 'And don't be shy. Or nervous, for that matter. You're not nervous, are you? I don't make you nervous, do I?'

Rocco enjoyed the way she blushed, the way the girl was so easy to entice out from behind the persona of the businesswoman—a persona that didn't fit nearly as snugly as she maybe imagined. At least, not to him. 'I just don't get why you're here, working at Hailey's. It's very pretty out here, but it's not exactly the centre of the universe for a young woman, especially one who had dreams of being somewhere else and doing something else.'

'I told you, I came because—'

'I know. There was no one else and you had to support your father.'

'My brother did come over but he could only stay for a very short while.'

'Why's that? Shouldn't it have been all hands to the pump?'

'Conor…he lives in Australia and he's married. He and his wife run a gym. He couldn't take more than a couple of weeks off. You know how it is, when you work for yourself.'

Ella felt something she seldom had before—a deep sense of unfairness. Was she being uncharitable? She felt tears prick the back of her eyes. She was just being human. Conor had come, and then in the blink of an eye he'd gone, and here she was all these months later, still picking up pieces, still being the dutiful daughter while Conor carried on…just being Conor.

'No. I don't.'

'What do you mean? Commitments…sometimes you can't spare the time when you might want to.'

'And did he want to? Because, from where I'm sitting, he sounds more than a little selfish. Surely he would have known that you would be putting your life on hold?'

And that was about the gist of it, wasn't it? A life put on hold—her life.

She didn't understand why she found it so easy to talk to this man. Was it because he was a stranger? Because he wouldn't be hanging around, so she would never have to face the consequences of anything said in confidence?

Or, deep down, had she simply been lonely after her mother died, and after the break-up that had been so painful? Did this guy just happen to have the key to open up a well of sadness she'd never properly acknowledged?

'I guess my kid brother's always been selfish.' Ella sighed. She propped her chin in the palm of her hand and looked at Rocco's beautiful, sympathetic face. Something inside her leapt, a thrill of succumbing to a feeling she wanted and was no longer going to resist, something that had been growing ever since she'd set eyes on him. 'My mum had cancer when we were both still at home and...well... I was always the serious one in the family, the dependable one. I was the good little girl and Conor was the one who got away with doing what he wanted.'

'I get it.'

'What? What do you get?'

Rocco didn't say anything for a couple of seconds. He'd never felt this engaged in a conversation with any woman in his life before but then, he reminded himself, he wasn't *Rocco*, he was *Jose*. Jose came with freedoms that Rocco had never had. Of course he would react in ways that were alien to the carefully controlled guy he'd always been!

'You never had your moment of rebellion because your brother was the one who did that and, for as long as he was the rebel, you subconsciously strove to be the one who kept things on an even keel, especially if your mother was chronically ill.'

'How did you just do that?'

She smiled, and for a second Rocco's heart swelled with pleasure. He wasn't the billionaire who ran an empire and gave orders to people who jumped when he spoke.

He was the kid who got the answer right in class in front of the girl he wanted to impress.

'Do what?'

'Get me to open up to you. I haven't said that to anyone but, yes, you're right. Conor was the rule breaker, and the more he broke the rules, the more I obeyed them. I suppose I thought that he could have stayed longer after mum died. He was helpful, and he arranged a lot of things while he was here, but then he was gone and here I am. I stayed.'

'But surely you didn't have to?'

'Why is this conversation all about me?' Ella glanced at the menu that seemed magically to appear in front of her and randomly chose something off it without really registering what she was ordering. She laughed but her laughter dried up at the depth of his dark gaze as it rested on her, questioning, thoughtful and breaking down yet more of those barriers she had erected.

'Maybe I fell into a rut.'

'Too much excitement out there? Easier to kick back and see where life decides to take you?'

But he was smiling when he said it, and she smiled shyly back at him.

'I needed to get away,' she said in a low, broken voice. 'I... I never thought I'd end up getting away for good. I always assumed I'd finish my geography degree, but then I came back here and day to day reality took over, and one day I realised that finishing my degree was no longer a priority. I guess... I fell into a rut of my own making.'

'You said that you needed to get away...'

'I... I'm boring you. I'm talking all about myself. You

must think I'm crazy to be sobbing on your shoulder when I don't even know you.'

'Maybe that's why you find it so easy.'

'Tell me about yourself.'

Their food had arrived, as if mysteriously, because Ella was so oblivious to everything around her, including the waiter who had refilled their wine glasses and presumably made the usual noises to ask what they wanted.

'What do you want to know?'

'Do you have any family? Brothers? Sisters? Cousins? Annoying uncles and aunts you only see at Christmas? Do you miss living in Spain, running your store there? Actually, you haven't really told me where you live... Do you live over here?'

Rocco lowered his eyes. Her open honesty was discomforting, reminding him why he was here in the first place, and honesty didn't play a big part. He squashed his niggling conscience fast. What was happening here wasn't about his acquisition of the store. What was happening here was about the two of them and their unlikely attraction.

'No brothers or sisters. An uncle, yes—not in touch. He's the black sheep of the family.'

'That's a shame,' Ella said with sympathy. 'Family is so important, and it doesn't sound as though you have lots to go round.'

'Can't say I've shed tears over that.'

'But there's always a reason that a black sheep is a black sheep, don't you think?'

'Haven't really thought about it.'

'Sometimes it's the family dynamic, having to live

up to a sibling who's cleverer or better-looking or the favourite…'

Rocco—who normally would have repelled that sort of mumbo jumbo—thought about what she'd said. He thought about his uncle and the steadiness of his own father—the cold confidence that had been in such stark contrast. They were rather like Ella and her brother, he thought, but so much more destructive with so much money and power at stake. There hadn't been room for a wild card, especially when the wild card had gone so far off the rails that he'd threatened to ruin the company.

'Maybe you're right, but hey, who needs the potted history?'

'I just gave you some of mine,' Ella pointed out.

'Far more interesting than mine. Tell me why you needed to get away, Ella. Your openness is sexy. I like it.'

Rocco relaxed. He was back on safe ground instead of uncomfortably skirting round the truth about who he was and why he was here.

'I fell in love,' Ella said simply. She laughed a little self-consciously. 'At university. I fell in love with a guy and I thought he'd fallen in love with me as well.' She raised her eyes to his and wiped her mouth on her serviette. What had she just eaten? It had been very tasty but she couldn't say. 'I don't know why I'm telling you all this stuff.'

'You know why. We're ships passing in the night. We can say whatever we want and do whatever we want because nothing will come back to bite us in the future.'
Also true. And this was why he felt so liberated, why he

wasn't watchful with her, or keeping her at an emotional at arm's length.

'Tell me,' he said roughly.

'It's all history now, but I suppose it's why I stayed here. Deep down, maybe I was afraid to return to my course, afraid to bump into Steve. He was studying geography as well. We bonded over our passion about climate change. At least, that's what I thought at the time.'

'But instead…?'

She laughed, faltering. 'Instead, it turned out that he went out with me because he wanted to bond with my best friend. Actually, he wanted to do a lot more than bond with her. Or, rather, he *did* want to bond…in a very, *very* literal way. He used me to get to her, and she decided he was a better catch than the guy she was dating, who was messing her around. I was collateral damage and neither of them looked back.'

'Ella…'

'No need to feel too sorry for me,' she said lightly. 'Everybody has to have a little heartbreak in their life now and again, and I'm well and truly over him.'

Rocco felt a jolt of pain on her behalf. He felt submerged in her story in a way he would never have dreamed possible. Her sweet, heart-shaped face was a picture of the stiff upper lip as she recounted something that had clearly been shattering for her at a time when she'd been going through the grief of losing her mother.

'If that man was sitting here right now, I'd wring his neck.'

This time her laugh was genuine. 'You're sweet.'

'I'm the opposite of sweet,' Rocco growled.

'But you're not.' She reached across, gently touched his hand and, when he linked his fingers with hers, she squeezed them and smiled. 'I thought you were the most arrogant guy I'd ever met when you waltzed into my office.'

'I'm extremely arrogant.'

'But underneath all that arrogance and self-confidence there's a really sweet guy who knows how to listen, and is genuine and honest.'

Rocco flushed darkly. 'I break hearts.'

'My heart isn't on the line here.'

'Good,' Rocco said in a low, driven voice. 'Because...'

'Because?'

'I want you, Ella. I want to take you to bed and make love to you until you're crying out for more. But I don't want to end up hurting you in the process.'

A thread of reckless abandon stole into her. She'd spent her entire life being careful and the oppressive weight of that was something she had always kept to herself. She had never really thought about it...until now.

Just when she'd least expected it, this stranger had come into her life and thrown everything into focus. He'd made her see things she might not have wanted to see, but she couldn't *un*-see them. She didn't like the trajectory of her life, didn't like the way she'd run away and then hadn't really stopped running, even though she could have a while back.

He was dangerous. She felt it. He was arrogant, self-confident, empathetic, strong: *a potent mix*. But did she care how dangerous he was? She could withstand that potent mix because she could never go for a guy like him; could never be sucked in to emotional involvement with someone who was so far out of her comfort zone. She was too grounded, whatever temporary recklessness was possessing her.

'I… I've never done anything… I'm not the sort of girl… You're saying these things…'

'We both know why we're here, having dinner. This is foreplay, and we both want what comes next. You're still young, Ella,' Rocco said with cool, gentle persuasion in his voice. 'Give yourself permission to live a little, whatever heartbreak you've suffered. Or else the creep who broke your heart wins.'

'Yes, well…'

'Sometimes,' Rocco murmured, leaning forward and tugging her into him, 'It doesn't pay to be too careful. You spend so long dodging land mines that you forget there's a world out there where land mines don't exist. You forget how to live the life you have.'

Ella breathed, looking at the dark intent on his face. 'And sometimes you get out there and forget that you might just step on a land mine you hadn't expected because you got a little too complacent. And when that happens…it's all over.'

'Trust me—I won't be one of those annoying errant land mines, Ella.' He smiled slowly, flipped her hand over and traced tiny circles on the sensitive underside of her wrist. He held her gaze. 'You know what you're getting with me—no nasty surprises. What we'll have is fun for a week or so and then I'll disappear from your life.'

'No nasty surprises…'

'None. I'll leave. And when I do…' he smiled. '…you won't regret that I've been…'

CHAPTER THREE

WOULD SHE REGRET IT? Could she trust him? He'd smiled that slow, lazy, utterly charming smile and she'd blinked away all her doubts. She'd forgotten her vows to be careful after Steve. She'd relegated to oblivion all her resolutions about only letting any man into her life when she knew that he could be trusted.

'You should take a few days off,' he'd said, as they'd left the restaurant hand in hand, heading for the place he had rented on the outskirts of town. 'I want you to myself while I'm here and shadowing you is going to get in the way of that. Unless there are private cubby holes where we can hide…?'

'You can't do that!'

'Why not?'

'Because…you're here for a fortnight! You've signed up to work.'

'I'm not on a pay roll.' He'd shrugged. 'And I'm okay with trading some of my time here for more pleasurable pastimes. Live on the wild side, Ella—forget about duty for a minute.' He'd pulled her against him and kissed her, and that kiss had been devastating. He'd looked her in the eyes, sifting his fingers through her hair and cupping her face. 'And that means not finding excuses to be careful all the time. I'm not as poor as you think, even if I happen to be your slave for a fortnight.'

'Hardly a slave!'

'Don't knock it. I like the thought of you giving me orders. Take the rest of the week off. I'll book us somewhere—a cottage. We can play house until I leave next weekend.'

'Play house?'

'By that,' he'd clarified quickly, 'I mean lie in bed all day and only get up to shower or eat.'

He'd rented a cottage... *What had he expected?* He'd taken time out with women before—a five-star hotel somewhere in a bustling city. He travelled extensively and occasionally had a woman travel with him. If she disliked falling in line and taking second billing to his work commitments, then nothing had ever been said, because he'd lavished her with expensive gifts and taken her to classy restaurants. Money was always a great persuader.

Now, though... He'd had his EA find a suitably rustic cottage buried in the countryside. She'd emailed a picture of it and Rocco had given her the go-ahead. It was nothing Rocco Mancini would have contemplated in a million years, but as soon as they'd reached it, it had felt right.

Two days on, it still felt right. There were no expensive shops, no expensive restaurants, no expensive gifts bought. There was just a cottage in the middle of nowhere, nestled in rolling green hills.

'Need a hand?'

Rocco was sprawled on the deep, old-fashioned sofa watching as Ella busied herself in the kitchen. They were playing house. It wasn't something he'd done before in his life but he was doing it now and enjoying it. Outside, the fading sun was casting the last shadows over a garden bursting with wild flowers. Inside, the furnishings were cosy and worn, with lots of throws on the chairs and sofa, wooden beams on the ceiling and a central stone fireplace that dominated the living area.

Ella looked across at Rocco lying on the sofa, ankles loosely crossed and one hand behind his head, the other dangling to the side. It was a little after six and her body still tingled from when they had made love only a couple of hours before. She felt dampness spread between her legs and knew from the slow smile he shot her that he could read exactly what she was thinking.

I want you. Ella couldn't believe how far she'd come from the cautious girl who had resented having someone rearrange her work pattern by showing up without warning in her carefully ordered office to the girl she was now: open, free and trusting. She'd taken one look at the cottage he had rented for the week and had known that this was a guy who *got her.*

'What would you like to help me with?' she teased now, strolling towards him with a knife in one hand and an onion in the other.

'I can't have a conversation with you when you're approaching me with a knife. A man can get a little edgy around a woman with a knife.'

Ella burst out laughing. Yes, he got her. Got her in ways she had never expected. He made her laugh with his dry wit and listened to her with dark, pensive eyes that encouraged her to confide, confide, confide.

'Would you know how to cook a meal?' she smiled, moving to sit next to him and then curling into him as he adjusted his big body so that she could fit neatly into him.

'I can rustle up something edible if I have no choice.'

'Honestly, Jose, for a guy who lives on his own, I'm shocked that you're not more proficient in front of a cooker. I guess you get women to cook for you?'

Now and again, Ella noted little things that made her think, like ripples quietly disturbing the calm surface of a lake. Such as the fact that she knew precious little about him aside from the basics. Of course, she reasoned, she didn't need someone's entire back story to know that they were right for her; that they were kind, good and fair. He'd told her to have an adventure, to live in the moment, and that was what she was doing. She was following his lead, stepping out of her comfort zone and enjoying it.

Except...time was moving on and now, nestled against him, feeling his heartbeat through his tee shirt, she wondered where things were going. Time felt in short supply and suddenly she had a pressing urge to find out more about him, to make the connection between them stronger.

Maybe to know whether there was room for them to develop what they'd started after he left...?

Her heart fluttered. She'd told herself that she was in control of a situation that brought her physical satisfaction without emotional entanglement, because her head told her he wasn't the sort of guy she was looking for. Not as a long-term proposition.

After Steve, she told herself she would be careful. She based her benchmark on her dad, who was quietly strong, reliable and kind, a man of few words who knew what it was like to devote his life to the woman he loved. He and her mother had adored one another. He'd been her rock and had been there for her through the many years of uncertain health.

That was what she was looking for. Not a guy who made her body sing, who took her to places she'd never imagined possible but who was also the essence of charm, easy wit and stunning self-assurance.

Yet…she couldn't quite imagine life without him in it, and that scared her. Was there a connection there for him as well? He wasn't taking a risk like she was. So was this just another every-day fling for him? Or more than that?

'I don't, actually.'

'So you cook for yourself? Tell me what you like to cook.'

'That's a lot of questions.'

'I want to find out more about you. You know so much about me. I've never confided in anyone the way I've confided in you, and I'm not even sure how you've managed to get me to tell you so much.'

'I'm a persuasive kind of guy,' Rocco murmured.

'I can't actually believe I'm here with you.'

'Yet how hard was it to tell your manager that you wanted a few days off? And I'm still not sure why you had to skirt around the reason for that by saying I'd had to cut short my stint there, and you needed a break to regroup from having your routine put out of sync by my unexpected presence.'

'People have a way of gossiping.'

'Does it matter what people think?'

'It does to me.'

'Why?'

'I suppose,' Ella said thoughtfully, 'That it's just the way I've always been. I've always been quite restrained. Like I've told you, Conor was the one who took up all the oxygen. He demanded attention and, the more he demanded, the more I retreated into myself. Especially with Mum—having to deal with health issues that cropped up time and again. I felt like the last thing my parents needed was the headache of two kids testing the boundaries.'

'Did you ever resent that?'

'Until I met you, it wasn't something I'd ever confronted. It was what it was. You're the only one who knows just how awful my experience with Steve was. I lost a future I thought I might have with him, but it was more than that. Because of what he did, I lost my friend as well.'

'People like that don't deserve your friendship or your love.'

Rocco could smell the sweet, floral scent of her hair and, as he breathed it in, he felt the tight, grim throb of rage when he thought about the guy who'd let her down, because she hadn't deserved that.

It wasn't jealousy. He didn't do jealousy. He never had. But, in a way, it was worse than jealousy, because it was a sort of possessiveness and that was alien to him. He almost wished he'd been around at the time to protect her from a guy who should have been kicked out of her life before he'd got his foot through the door.

What was *that* about? Why wasn't he more concerned at how intimate they had become in such a short time?

He was a man who guarded his emotions, who never encouraged women to over-share and who was happy to have sex as the motivator behind relationships, safe in the knowledge that when the time came to take a wife he would only ever consider one who logically fitted the bill. Emotion would play no part in his choice.

But this unusual freedom…life in the guise of someone else, intimacy…didn't feel like a threat. He enjoyed her soft murmurings as she confided in him, told him things that were close to her heart. It made him want to talk to her as well.

'Have you ever lost your heart to someone?' he heard her ask.

'Not my style.'

'You're in your thirties and you've never lost your heart to anyone?'

'I…' Rocco hesitated, knowing that there was a limit to what he could tell her but also knowing that, within those limits, there was a lot he could confide, and it shocked him just how much he wanted to do that.

'Go on. I'm open with you.'

'You *are* very open,' he agreed. 'Sometimes, it feels as though you're from another planet.' He smiled when she laughed. 'In a good way. You tell me about yourself and you're not trying to impress me.'

'Women try to impress you? No, don't answer that. I can well imagine. Is that why you're so self-confident?'

'You can well imagine? I like that. Very good for my ego.' Rocco kissed the crown of her head and sifted his fingers through her hair, tilting her face to his and then very gently contouring her lips with his tongue so that she shivered against him and came a little closer.

He thought about his background: extreme wealth, extreme privilege, the very foundations of inbuilt self-confidence. He wondered how she would react if he were to come clean, but that wasn't an option, and if there was a twinge of unease at the thought of what he was obliged to keep to himself then he dismissed it because they were both in a bubble, far removed from reality. He would leave, she would return to being the person she was and it would be the same for him. Ships passing in the night.

'Maybe,' she mused, 'You're confident because you're an only child, so you've never had to tailor your personality to adapt to a sibling, and you've never had to compete for your parents' attention. You must have been lavished with love.'

'Actually,' Rocco said pensively, 'I wouldn't say that I was very close to my parents at all.'

'Weren't you?'

She levered herself up and stared at him with undisguised curiosity, which made him smile again.

'They were very cold.'

'Why? Poor you.' She hugged him and held him tightly for a couple of seconds. 'You must have been lonely as an only child if your parents were distant. Were you?'

'I... I suppose,' Rocco said slowly, 'There were times when I was. Yes.'

'When?'

'You ask a lot of questions, don't you?' He breathed in deeply, and there it was again—a feeling of freedom that he knew he would treasure when life returned to normal and he resumed his responsibilities. 'Christmas.'

'Christmas?'

Rocco burst out laughing. 'For someone who's been through quite a bit, you're very soft-hearted. Yes, Christmas was never the highlight of my life.'

'My family was always very close. My brother may have been a little wild—' she smiled '—but there was never any question that we were there for one another. I feel for you when you tell me that you weren't close to your parents and were lonely at Christmas…that's a joyous time of the year. It's a big deal here and at Hailey's. We hold a lunch for people who are homeless and we arrange a Santa grotto for the kids. The store sponsors it all.'

Rocco didn't want to think about Hailey's because it reminded him of the fate that awaited it. It was also an unwelcome reminder that this liberated man wasn't him but someone else, someone on borrowed time, someone the real Rocco would look back on with affection and bemusement.

'Don't feel too sad for me,' he breathed, his body stirring into arousal as the feel of her against him became too much to bear. 'I got presents and there was a tree. It was just never celebrated with any warmth. What's happening with that food? Can it wait? Because I can't.'

He touched her, relaxing into the less challenging place where physical contact took precedence over touchy-feely conversation that was so unlike him.

'I like talking to you,' Ella murmured. 'You're nothing like what I expected when they told me that someone would be coming to shadow me for a fortnight.'

'And you're nothing like what I expected when I came here. I never thought that my boss would be a woman who drove me crazy with desire. Let's stop talking. I want to make love to you.'

Ella wound her arms round his neck and smiled when he hoisted her easily off the sofa and took her into the bedroom. She wasn't wearing a bra or any underwear. She'd quickly become accustomed to the way he wanted to touch her all the time, scooping down into her soft jogging bottoms to feel the wetness between her legs or pulling her towards him and pushing up her jumper so that he could caress her breasts. He'd told her that he'd quite like her to walk around completely naked in the cottage but, failing that, to dispense with the underwear. From the stern position of never making the mistake of yielding to any man, she had yielded to those demands with lightning speed.

Thoughts left her head in a hurry. She lay back on the bed and watched as he stripped off, as mesmerised by the muscled strength of his body as though she was seeing it for the first time. He was exquisite—broad-shouldered and narrow-hipped, muscular but athletic, as though he worked out, even though he'd told her in passing that he never went to a gym because he hated the thought of committing to a certain amount of exercise a week.

She tugged off her clothes, first the jogging bottoms and then the tee-shirt, and flung both on the floor. He strolled towards the bed and her legs parted of their own volition. She was so wet for him, so ready for him to settle over her.

The curtains weren't drawn and fading light filtered

in, mellow and warm on the wood panelling and whitewashed stone. As soon as Ella had stepped into the cottage, she'd felt at home. It was warm and cosy, with timbered beams across low ceilings and faded rugs on the floor. There was an open fireplace in the bedroom and a basket of logs next to it, ready for winter. As Rocco caressed her, she idly wondered what it would be like if they were here in winter, snow falling and the feel of Christmas all around them.

She relaxed into that fantasy but that, too, flew from her head as he began a slow exploration of her body until all she wanted to do was writhe against those searching fingers. Years of her careful life were swept away in a torrent of explosive desire that was ripping her apart. She burned up as his hand moved from her small breasts to between her legs, rubbing the flat of his fingers against the swollen bud of her clitoris. Each stroke of those clever fingers ratcheted up the scorching heat of her responsive body.

His touch felt familiar but no less arousing, and she groaned, eyelids fluttering, her body moving as he caressed her between her sprawled legs. His nakedness was hot against her and she reached to circle his thick member with her hand so that she could stroke him, picking up the tempo, knowing exactly how he liked to be touched because he had been shockingly open about telling her.

She slowly bucked against his fingers, an orgasm building to sweep her away. It took all her willpower to fight it, to push his hand away so that she could devote herself to ministering to *him*, to pleasuring *him*. He was a generous lover, satisfying her before himself, taking his time when she knew that he was on the edge of exploding. He was the sort of lover who made her feel *loved*. Although, of course, this wasn't about *love*.

She angled her body and laughed when he tried to pin her down, but he was happy enough to lie back, to let her touch him, then lowering herself along his brown, hard body, down to his penis, which she licked and stroked before taking it into her mouth. She lost herself in the taste and the urgent throb of him as she sucked and felt the pump of blood in his veins, the pulsing response of a man who, like her, was lost in a world of sensory pleasure.

He detached from her with a low, guttural moan and fumbled blindly for the packet of condoms he had stashed in the drawer next to the bed. Not a guy to take chances. She was giddy with arousal. She wanted him to touch her again but knew that, if he did, she wouldn't be able to control the fevered urgency of her response and she didn't want to come against his hand. She wanted him inside her.

She closed her eyes and controlled her breathing, waiting for his body to merge with hers and for the yearning inside her to be sated. He thrust into her in one powerful motion that took her breath away and he began moving inside her, his rhythm deep and forceful until she could feel her whole body spiralling out of control in ways that were mind-blowing. She came on a cry of deep pleasure and flung back her head. Her mouth was open while her eyes were squeezed tightly shut. How was it possible to feel this depth of pure, joyful, satisfying, earth-shattering, wondrous pleasure?

She knew when he had come, his orgasm mirroring hers. She could feel him swell inside her, filling her up.

She was oblivious to everything but the heat of her excited body as it slowly descended from the crescendo of her orgasm back down to planet Earth. She sagged against him and, for a few moments, neither of them said anything.

'I feel as though we've known one another for ever.' Ella broke the silence with a dreamy murmur. She held back the thought that followed: that she felt she knew this man after a few days so much better than she'd ever known Steve. Felt that he knew *her* a thousand times better than Steve had, and yet how was that possible? With Steve, she'd had hopes and plans for a future, yet it seemed restrained and limiting compared to the pure heady freedom she felt with this man, who was practically a stranger.

Wasn't he? Or was this what a *real connection* felt like—impossibly close, entwined, on the same wavelength? Was this what *true love* felt like? Love that wasn't a slow build but a rush of everything good all at once? Her heart began a steady beat inside her. *He was going.* He hadn't said anything at all about prolonging his stay.

'How so?'

She warmed as he drew her closer. She rested her palm on his chest and felt his heartbeat, and a rush of love swept through her, leaving her weak, warm and giddy.

'I feel like a different person when I'm with you,' she confessed truthfully. 'I feel adventurous and I don't think I've ever felt adventurous in my whole life.'

'You've cocooned yourself here, and I understand. You were grieving for your mother, you were hurt from a broken love affair and it felt safe to be here where there's nothing to stretch you.'

'That's true, but it's more than that. I've always toed the line but this feels...different. You've brought out a side to me I never thought existed. Have I...have I done that for you as well?'

Rocco remained silent for a few seconds. He felt lazy and comfortable with her body against his, the smell and feel of her filling him. He shifted so that he was facing her, her breasts against his chest and his thigh tucked between her legs. He was Jose Rivero, here in this cottage with this woman in his arms. If the question might have felt intrusive in another life, in *this* life, the one where the weight of duty no longer existed, the answer was yes. He felt a different man.

For just a second, that fleeting thought was enough to send ripples of discomfort through him. But why should it, he asked himself, when he was going to be leaving in a matter of...?

A couple of days.

Rocco frowned at the tug somewhere deep inside him at the prospect of leaving. There'd been times when he'd almost forgotten why he was here in the first place! When he returned to reality, he would laugh at that and shake his head in disbelief.

'Brought out a side to me I never thought existed? Now, let me think about that. You've certainly brought out a sexual side to my nature I never thought could be so powerful.'

'You know what I mean. I'm not talking about the sex. When it comes to sex, well, that's a whole new conversation. I barely recognise the woman who's happy to walk around without any underwear and wants to be touched whenever and wherever.'

'You've led a sheltered life.' He grinned but actually found that he loathed thinking about her with the guy who'd later let her down. 'If I'd been around during your formative years, walking around without underwear would have been the least adventurous streak in you.' He thought of her as a young girl, quiet and thoughtful, making sure never to be the centre of attention. He would like to have been there for her, which was a crazy notion.

'You have such a big ego, Jose Rivero!'

Rocco winced at the mention of his alter ego. He heard himself say with rough sincerity, 'I've certainly never done anything like this before. A cottage in the middle of nowhere, with a woman walking around barefoot in the kitchen cooking meals for me while I pick apples from the trees in the garden.'

Rocco reflected on his relationships with women, casual and satisfying enough, but nothing like this. Women he courted, wined, dined and slept with, knowing that he would marry someone whom logic dictated would fit the bill: someone from his own class who understood what came with the job of being his wife.

'So I'm a first?'

'In many ways.'

Ella sighed with contentment as he stroked her back, his fingers tracing her spine light and ticklish. She liked the sound of him telling her she'd been a first. She wasn't going to say anything about how she felt; she was going to obey the invisible lines she thought were in place because, realistically, he hadn't once talked about a future.

Did he want more from them? He had worked a steady path into her heart but the residue of disillusionment from the way she and Steve had crashed and burned was still there. Yes, she had fallen straight into him, maybe against her better judgement, but part of Ella recognised the danger of letting go of all the barriers she had built up around herself.

But the thought of him walking out of her life in a matter of days made her blood run cold. For better or for worse, she had to find out where things stood between them. She had to know whether there was a chance he had feelings for her which he maybe hadn't even acknowledged, because it sure wouldn't have been part of his plan when he'd arrived at Hailey's.

'I can't think of any woman who's managed to distract me from work the way you have,' he said and Ella smiled against his chest.

'I don't believe you.'

'Work is part and parcel of who I am.'

'Yet here you are.'

'Yet here I am.'

'What happens to your store when you want to go on holiday? I know you've told me you have people who can take over, but surely you must relax now and again?'

'I play as hard as I work.'

'And yet you've never taken this sort of time out? Where do you go when you want to unwind? I understand how you've had to be focused on your job if you've had to build something from nothing. Working for yourself is always going to be a big ask—not much time to relax if you know that a week off might mean less money in the bank.'

'Times aren't quite that hard for me,' Rocco murmured uncomfortably. He flushed as the reality of who he was collided with the person she thought he was…and yet this wasn't game he was playing. For a moment in time, while he was here with her, he truly felt a different man—carefree and reckless, without the layers of control that, by definition, restricted a lot of his responses. It wasn't going to last, of course. Reality was something he could never ditch, not that he would ever want to do that.

'And when it comes to the sort of things I do to unwind…'

'No gym.'

'You remembered. No, that sort of regime doesn't suit me. I do get away now and again, but this is the first time I haven't been overly concerned about checking in to see what's happening at…er…work…'

Skirting around the truth heightened his discomfort, and instead he told her with surprising honesty, 'I've always been a very controlled person, even in my relationships with women. You…bring out a different side to me. Now, what's happening about food? We could venture out and eat somewhere.'

'I've already started doing something for us to eat.'

'Sure you don't want to be wined and dined?' Rocco thought about how satisfying that would be—to take her out somewhere fancy, to impress her. Was this the road his uncle had travelled, step by step, until he couldn't get off it? Had his problems started with an infantile desire to impress a woman unused to the seductive aphrodisiac of extreme wealth? This lack of self-control was so unlike him that he struggled to dismiss it as just a reaction to being in the unique position of a woman not knowing his worth.

His mind continued to play with the fantasy of her in his private jet, sitting in one of his many cars or being taken to one of his villas—one in Tuscany, one in the Bahamas and another on the outskirts of Madrid.

He looked around him at the quaint, rustic furnishings. The wooden beams on the ceiling matched the timber of the four-poster bed: old, weathered and gnarled. The windows were fiddly but, when they were open, the scent of the countryside poured into the bedroom, fragrant and heady.

There was no *en suite*. The one bathroom had an old-fashioned shower and a bath with clawed feet, as deep as a swimming pool. Filling it, which they had only done once, was a procedure that had to be commenced at least half an hour before they even thought about getting in.

This was a place the twenty-first century hadn't quite decided whether to visit or not. And now Rocco could say, hand on heart, that his enjoyment of it was every bit as complete as his enjoyment of any one of his splendid, eye-wateringly expensive places scattered across the globe.

He frowned as he quickly replayed the many confidences they had shared, bit by bit, and the way he had relaxed in her company, so that now she felt familiar to him. He barely recognised the man who had opened up in ways he'd never done before. She'd awakened in his arms in the morning, warm and smiling, and there had been dreamless times at night when they had made love, both half-asleep, their movements slow, languorous and incredibly sensual. Rocco was alarmed now at how natural everything seemed with her.

'This is perfect,' he heard her say, all the while trying to analyse the road he had travelled down so quickly it was shocking.

'Let's stop talking,' he growled, hand straying to part her thighs then cupping and rubbing the wetness between them until she was moaning softly and sighing, her body moving against his hand while she did some exploring of her own.

He slipped his finger inside her, then his hands and fingers caressed her until her soft moaning became the guttural groans of a woman on the point of orgasm.

'Not so fast,' he purred silkily when he knew she was on the verge of tipping over the edge.

'Please...'

'I love it when you beg, *querida*...but I need to be inside you...' He fumbled, found the packet of condoms and was vaguely startled by the quantity left when it felt as though they'd made love a thousand times over the past few days. He was losing his touch in a million different ways.

He cleared his head and found his sweet spot, the place where niggling thoughts ceased to exist, found the comfort of touch.

'We don't have much more time together.' The words had to be spoken; he knew that. Yet, they cut deep inside him. 'Let's make the most of it...'

CHAPTER FOUR

'THE BIG GUY—and I mean *Mr Big himself*—wants to see you right now, in the boardroom. And, before you ask, he's *specifically* asked for *you*.'

Ella was barely through the front doors of the department store, sodden, because she'd had to half-run from her car in lightly falling snow. She decided that her stress levels must surely have peaked with this.

'Why?'

'Believe me, I'm mystified as well—unplanned visit. I took a call from whatever assistant he's brought with him asking for you *by name*. Now he has free rein of the store, the lawyers have been in. He's been here since seven this morning. He's yet to be seen by any of us lesser mortals. Easier to spot a leprechaun.'

'Probably ashamed, turning the store into yet another office block and high-end apartments for yuppies who work in Dublin. And at Christmas too! What a time to tell everyone they're being laid off so enjoy earning money while they can.'

'It's awful.' Vera sighed. 'But there's nothing to be done and word has it that he's been more than fair with everyone working here. Generous redundancies or new jobs in what's going up, if they're qualified for the placement. We all knew, even if we didn't want to admit it, that things were going downhill. It's not such a shock.'

'So why does he want *me*? I'm not involved in the decision making. I'm not a lawyer or an accountant so what have I got to say to the man?'

Ella finally got her feet to move. She noticed how old and tired everything looked as she took off her waterproof and shook it out. None of this was Vera's fault, but once again hormones had taken over and directed her responses.

She was right. Once a proud bastion of high-end glamour and luxury, the store had been declining slowly over the years. There had been murmurings but nothing definite until, out of the blue, it was announced that the place had been taken over and would be restructured into a massive block of very expensive apartments, with the entire top floor given over to office space.

Maybe at any other time she could have dealt with it, but right now what Ella wanted more than anything else was continuity, and the store's imminent closure had hit her like a hammer blow.

Vera was looking at her through shrewd, narrowed eyes and Ella smiled and sighed. 'Okay, okay. I'm fine. I'll go and see him just as soon as I get my act together. I've barely had time to take a breath.'

'I know things are tough at the moment, Els…'

'I don't want to talk about it. You've been good enough already, listening to me on a loop.'

'It's what friends do.'

'Tell Mr Big that I'll be in the boardroom in fifteen

minutes. And Vera...?' Ella grinned, for a moment the girl once again instead of the woman with the weight of the world on her shoulders. 'You don't have to worry. I'll make sure the hormones are firmly under lock and key, whatever the man has to say.'

Three floors up, Rocco was seated at the sprawling conference table, gazing at nothing, with his thoughts all over the place. Yet somewhere deep inside, for the first time in months, he felt at peace.

The last time he'd been here, the sun had been shining and the skies were the milky blue of fading summer. Now, the onset of deep winter was making itself felt. It was bitterly cold, and through the bank of windows he could see the lazy flurry of snow, not quite sufficient to collect but enough to signal worse to come.

There was no need to be here. When he and Ella had parted company, it had been for good. They'd had a brief fling, nothing more. Towards the very end, he had felt the whisper of something just out of reach, emotions that could have led to an involvement that his practical side knew would never happen. She had looked at him and he had seen something that had set the alarm bells ringing.

More than that, he had sensed something inside himself, something that wasn't welcome, a pull that had begun to feel dangerously out of control. He had laid down his boundaries without hesitating, had reminded her that this was just a moment in time and then, on schedule, he had left.

By then, he'd known exactly what he would offer for the building and exactly how he would reconfigure it. He had seen the quality of the staff and acknowledged that he would be more than happy to offer alternative positions to some of them.

With everything nicely in motion, and planning permission smoothly progressing just as it should, there was absolutely no need for him to do anything more than sit back and oversee developments. His vast empire, with all the responsibilities that entailed, barely allowed him time to surface, far less make an unnecessary trip back to where…

Back to where he had left behind a piece of himself he had never known existed. That was the persistent thought that had nagged at him ever since he had left. Rocco had papered that over by telling himself that an uneasy conscience at withholding the truth from Ella was at the root of his restlessness since he'd returned to normal life. He'd get past it.

He hadn't. She'd played in his head like the refrain of a song he couldn't quite manage to forget. Why? He was always so adept when it came to women, always so controlled with what he gave and what he didn't. Emotions had never impacted on his behaviour but he'd found it impossible not to think about her.

So here he was. The chemistry between them had obviously been more powerful than he'd anticipated. What they'd shared hadn't burnt out and maybe it needed to be re-visited. It didn't mean there was anything serious between them. It just meant that an itch remained that needed to be scratched, and the choice was either to confront that by returning to face her or to pretend it didn't exist, which ran the risk of making the whole situation even more insupportable.

Reduced to the most basic level, Rocco reckoned that if something hadn't reached burnout, living in a state of denial wouldn't get it there any time soon. If he still felt this peculiar craving then chances were high that she did as well.

But he still felt ridiculously nervous as he waited for the knock on the door that would signal her arrival. And ridiculously excited at the prospect of how she would react when she saw him. Surprised? Dismayed? And, underneath whatever those initial reactions might be, excited at seeing him again? Bone-deep self-confidence settled on excitement.

He strolled towards the window, gazed down at the street below and then tensed as he heard the soft push of the door being opened.

Ella made it to the boardroom several minutes late but, frankly, she couldn't care. When she'd first been told about the sale of Hailey's she'd been more devastated than she'd thought possible. She'd known that the place needed an injection of cash, and that there had been chatter about it being sold for a while, but the reality of it had hit her for six. It was as if a tidal wave of memories and nostalgia had crashed into her with full force, sweeping her off her feet.

She'd wanted to confront whoever it was that had bought the store and tell him just how important it was for the town. But that outraged feeling hadn't lasted long because she'd known that whatever she had to say on the matter would fall on deaf ears. They'd been presented with a fait accompli and they would all have to live with it.

She pushed open the door and it took her a couple of seconds to focus on the figure standing with his back to her, staring out of the window in dark charcoal-grey trousers and white shirt cuffed to the elbows, and she noticed a jacket slung over the back of a chair.

He was very tall and dark-haired and, if something about him felt familiar, then she subconsciously dismissed the feeling because it was evident from the calibre of his clothing that this was the billionaire at the helm of the buyout. She was curious as to why he'd asked to see her but not nervous. Nothing the man said or did could possibly have any impact on her whatsoever.

'You asked to see me?'

Her voice echoed in the cavernous boardroom. She was standing by the door, focusing on the towering figure as he slowly turned to look at her.

Reality took a hundred years to catch up with disbelief and, even when her brain screamed that the guy now looking at her was the same guy who had disappeared without a trace, she still froze in shock, finding it impossible to believe.

It was impossible to believe because it just *couldn't* be happening.

'Ella...'

That voice...deep, dark and seductive...

Ella closed her eyes and every bone in her body went limp as she felt herself falling, falling, falling...in a desperate attempt to escape the reality she had just been confronted with.

She came to groggily, lying on the uncomfortable sofa against the wall with a cushion propped under her head.

'Here. Drink this. It should be something stronger,' that sexy, familiar voice said. 'My preference would be a shot of brandy but unfortunately this is all on offer.'

'No,' Ella whispered. 'This can't be happening.'

'You're in shock. Drink some water. You need a couple of seconds to gather your thoughts.'

'Who *are* you? Jose? I don't understand. What are you doing here? No. No, no, no...' She closed her eyes and heard her shallow breathing whilst feeling his gaze on her. He was still there when she opened her eyes a moment later.

'I'm Rocco Mancini. I'm going to pull a chair over. Don't try and stand; you'll probably fall over. You're still weak. There's some food on the sideboard, so I'll bring you something to eat.'

'You...you can't be. You...'

'Wait. Don't move a muscle.'

'I'm not hungry!'

'You need to get some strength up. Stay right there.'

Where the heck was she going to go? Fly through the window? Sprint out through the door to the nearest lift?

She was as weak as a kitten and all the weaker when she contemplated what was now in the process of unfolding. Her hand snaked down to her stomach with its barely-there bump, not at all noticeable under the layers of warm clothing, the vest, jumper, waterproof gilet and trousers with the helpful elasticated waist.

After nearly four months, Ella had become accustomed to the reality of her pregnancy. It had taken a while, even though she had known within a month of Jose leaving that she was pregnant. At first, she had just *missed* him. There had been a hole in her heart that was wrenchingly painful to endure. Any repercussions of their love-making hadn't registered at all and she'd barely noticed that her period was late. Then she had. About the same time as she'd realised that she'd gone off coffee and noticed that her breasts were tender.

And yet, when she'd done that pregnancy test, held that little stick and saw those two bright lines, she'd still been shocked. She had still felt the blood rush to her face and the race of her pulse.

God, she'd done her best to find him, but she'd had nothing to go on. She'd given him her mobile number, but it didn't take her long to realise that the favour hadn't been returned, and from there all her belief in what they'd had had collapsed like a house of cards. She'd done the unthinkable and fallen for a guy who had treated her in a way she'd hoped never to be treated again. He'd disappeared without a backward glance, making sure to leave no footprints in the sand behind him.

She poured her heart out to him and told him stuff she'd never told anyone in her life before.

She'd told him about Steve and his betrayal, and had felt all fuzzy and warm when she'd heard the anger in his sympathetic, horrified reaction. And what had he gone and done? Had he been any better? Steve had lied about his intentions. He had dropped her without looking back. She'd trusted him the way she'd trusted Steve and he had let her down exactly as Steve had.

Was *she* the common denominator? Was there something inside her that attracted the man who couldn't be trusted? Common decency had dictated that she try to locate the man who had fathered the baby she was carrying. However bitter she had felt at him and his vanishing act, however hurt she had been by the way she had been treated, the guy was still the father of their baby and deserved to know.

In the end, with no leads, she had given up the search and accepted that she would be a single mum. She'd concluded that, even if she managed to track him down, he wouldn't want anything to do with a baby he hadn't asked for with a woman he hadn't wanted in his life for more than a week and a half.

She gathered herself and wriggled upright into a sitting position just as he reached out with a glass of water, which she ignored.

'So Jose Rivero never existed. Why did you pretend to be someone you weren't? Was it fun? Was it fun to string me along under a pseudonym? Were you laughing behind my back?'

In the heat of the moment, the horrifying business of the pregnancy faded into the background. Shock had quickly given way to a healthy dose of absolute burning rage at the curdled memory of the hurt she'd lived with for months.

'Ron Brisk-Hailey mentioned selling the department store some months ago. It was an off-the-cuff idea aired at a dinner party hosted by my parents at their place in Dubai, where Brisk-Hailey lives. The store has been losing money for years and he was propping it up with his personal fortune because it began life as a family concern.

He confessed that it was a situation that couldn't continue indefinitely, and he couldn't see a way out, because the option to buy everything online, especially after the pandemic, had become overwhelming.'

'Carry on,' Ella said tightly. 'I'm beginning to see where this might be going but I'd like you to spell it out for me anyway. Just in case I miss any juicy bits out.'

'He could have put the place out to public tender, but he was sentimental about its heritage and wanted to make sure his employees were well-treated. In turn, I needed to assess just how much the physical building was worth, never mind the value of the plot it stood on. We agreed that there would be no point spooking anyone on the off chance I decided not to go ahead with the purchase. I was ninety-nine percent there but there was still a chance that the missing one percent might break the deal.'

'At what point did you decide that it would be fun to sleep with me? In your make-believe role of ordinary person having a look around?'

'It wasn't my intention to get involved with anyone while I was here. I came to see what I was getting myself into, establish whether it would be worth the investment—make sure I offered a fair deal but didn't pay over the odds—and then I was going to leave and let my guys conclude business if I chose to go ahead.'

'I don't even recognise you. You look the same, you sound the same, but you're a stranger in expensive clothes who thought it was okay to lie to me. Was that because you had so little respect for me—you thought I didn't deserve the truth?'

'My hands were tied.'

Ella noted with grim satisfaction the dull flush that stole into his aristocratic face, although who knew whether he had a conscience or not?

'Then you should have thought twice about getting involved with someone you felt you had to lie to.'

'It was a two-way street, Ella. We were attracted to one another.'

'I was attracted to Jose Rivero—who never existed, as it turns out. I wasn't attracted to Rocco Mancini, a billionaire who was here to spy on everyone.'

'You're upset. I get that.'

'Do you? That's very big of you.' Her hand stole to her stomach and she balled it into a clenched fist because right now she had to think about what she was going to do and how she was going to do it. She felt sick at the thought of what happened next in a situation she had never banked on. Telling Jose Rivero that she was pregnant had seemed daunting enough. Breaking the news to this stranger in front of her, a billionaire with an agenda that had never included her, was terrifying.

'I understand why you're angry with me, but in actual fact I didn't have to make this trip. I came because I wanted to see you. And, yes, I didn't reveal my true identity...what happened between us was one hundred percent genuine.'

'In the grip of a guilty conscience? Why?' She tried and failed to mesh the Jose she'd given her heart to, the carefree, sexy man who had held her in his arms, with this powerful, wealthy stranger, looking at her with his head tilted to one side, dark eyes revealing nothing.

It was hopeless.

'Do you feel guilty about pretending to be someone you weren't? Or because you knew what an awful upheaval it would be for the department store to be sold to the highest bidder only interested in making even more money for himself?'

'I know the place means a lot to you, Ella. I know you worked here as a teenager. I know your mother worked here. There's an affection for it.'

'I wish I'd never told you any of that.' *More confidences thrown back in her face—yet another reminder of how gullible she'd been.*

'But you did.' Rocco raked his fingers through his hair and sighed. He sat forward, leaning towards her. 'Look, I didn't come here to explain away the decision to replace this store with something that actually makes sense. You know as well as I do that the place is losing money hand over fist and has been for a long time. The edifice will remain the same and it will be renovated to the highest of sustainable environmental standards. It will be the gold standard for other properties I plan to develop. As someone who wanted to explore climate change and sustainable lifestyles, you should approve of what I'm doing here.'

'Please don't remind me of all the things I told you that I shouldn't have,' Ella retorted with ice in her voice. 'Vera said that you explicitly asked to see me. Why, if not to give me weasly excuses for what you did?'

'Weasly?' Rocco's dark eyes flashed with outrage and in return Ella shot him a sneering look.

'That's right.'

'No one's ever called me "weasly" before!'

'You're a billionaire,' she snapped scornfully. 'Everyone's probably scared stiff of you.'

'Except you.'

Ella bristled in silence at this rejoinder. Their eyes met and tangled, and she felt the slow burn of something unwanted and intrusive. The memory of how he'd touched her seared through her anger. It was debilitating and unwelcome because it flew in the face of her bitter disillusionment at how things had turned out. How could she possibly feel anything for this stranger? But there was still this jarring, disturbing pull. She hated it.

'You asked me why I came back here, came back to see you. I returned because I couldn't get you out of my mind. I don't have a guilty conscience about my plans for the store because it'll be the best thing that could happen to the town. It'll bring people in, and they will be a motor for reviving the shops that haven't been doing well over the years. Hailey's isn't the only place that's been failing for some time.'

That all made sense, which was infuriating. The man she'd known had been hot, charming and passionate. The one sitting here in this boardroom was cool, logical and controlled.

But here was the inescapable link: he said that he hadn't been able to get her out of his mind...

Had he returned to tell her that—that he'd been thinking of her? Or, more likely, had he come so that they could reconnect—continue what they'd shared even though he hadn't had a problem walking out on her four months ago?

Had it turned out to be more difficult than he'd thought to airbrush her out? He was a very physical man. Whether he was Jose or Rocco, he was still the guy with a red-hot libido. Ella killed dead the warm swoop of pleasure at the thought that he might have missed her. There was so much more at stake than a simple case of a fling that hadn't worked out. He had deceived her. A man who deliberately withheld the truth about who he really was didn't qualify to be a responsible father, did he? If she turned him away now, would he shrug and disappear, having given it a go?

Ella knew that she could withhold the truth of the situation from him, just as he had withheld the truth of who he really was from her, and she was tempted. But a child deserved the best of both parents, for better or worse. She had had that luxury while he…had not. She remembered what he had said about Christmas, about how little it had meant to him. Another lie? Her gut feeling was that he'd been telling the truth when he'd said there had been some genuine connection between them, even though listening to her gut feelings hadn't done much for her in the past.

She needed to respond now and not react. She needed to know if her gut feeling was right, if he was a decent guy. If he'd felt he'd truly had no option but to keep the truth of his identity to himself, even after they'd become lovers, then he could still be prepared to stay for a bit to see how the bombshell of his buyout would affect everyone in the store.

It was Christmas. Whether it made sense for the store to be turned into flats or not, it had still been a body blow to staff lower down the pecking order who hadn't seen it coming. They would be compensated, but they'd been left shaken. If there was nothing in it for him, would he still stick around to find out how the people whose lives would change because of him might be feeling? Was there a shred of real caring in him or had she utterly misjudged him?

It was a stupid test. Ella knew that, but she was clinging to something that might shine a light on the crossroads at which she now was, stuck and helpless. She desperately wanted him to prove himself because there was a baby inside her and she needed to know the measure of him.

'If you came here to see if you could get me back into bed, then you can forget it, *Señor Mancini*. I have better things to do than re-visit a relationship with someone who didn't care enough to tell me the truth about himself.' It was clear from the lowering of his eyes that she had struck the jackpot in correctly assessing why he'd suddenly felt a need to connect. 'But...'

'But?'

'If you're here to show me that there's a side to you that's actually *caring*...that you bear some sort of resemblance to the man I thought you were...' She drew in a swift breath because she felt herself weaken at her own foolishness in falling for him. 'Then you would show that you cared about the people here.'

'I intend to be very fair,' Rocco said quietly. 'I've made sure that the redundancy packages are generous and there will be roles to fill when the offices are functioning. The pay will be much better than they could hope to earn working for the store. I'll be laying out the details of the deals in the new year but I hope to put minds to rest by assuring everyone that they will be treated fairly.'

'You could stay for a while and let everyone enjoy their

last Christmas here. We haven't even put up the usual tree in the foyer.'

'Yes, the Christmas tradition.' He flushed. 'You know how I feel about Christmas.'

'But this isn't *your* Christmas. This is the final Christmas spent here, at the store, and it should belong to everyone in the town before it disappears for ever.'

'I hear what you're saying, Ella.'

'You'll stay for at least a few days, be a presence here to stop jitters and ensure that everyone can leave this wonderful place with feelings of goodwill and optimism for what lies ahead?'

'It's good to see you,' Rocco murmured.

He smiled a slow, lazy smile, amused at the passion on her face, knowing that meeting her again had only reawakened his libido, which had been dormant since he had left this slice of unreality behind. She was just as he remembered: outspoken and tough to impress. Even now, knowing he was a billionaire, she hadn't wanted to hop into bed with him, hadn't been tempted by his money.

He'd stay. Would he be able to persuade her back into a relationship or had he blown it for good because he hadn't told her who he was? He could understand that but, even so, when cold common sense told him there was no reason to remain here, that he *was* being incredibly generous in his final package, he wanted to stay.

Just entering the department store earlier that morning, just returning to this part of the world, Rocco had suddenly felt...*different*. He'd returned to the life he'd left behind. Two weeks had changed him in ways he couldn't figure out; it had made him curious, and he didn't understand why because he'd always known just how dangerous curiosity could be. His uncle had been curious about all the wrong things, and look where that had got him.

But the feeling when he'd returned... Yes, he'd stay.

'You're really not tempted to pick up where we left off now that you've found out who I am?'

'I prefer the straightforward guy who could only afford to rent a small cottage.'

'I might have billions, Ella, but I'm still the same guy who knew how much you'd like it there.'

He liked the thought of her not wanting him because of his money. He played with the idea of her softening, coming to him, walking back into his arms. He thought of a different relationship with everything out in the open, although still one that would never amount to anything more than a fling, even if the fling lasted longer.

His thoughts on marriage didn't involve the sort of love she would expect, nor was she a woman from the elevated background that would prepare her for the life she would have to lead as his wife. Control would be the very essence of his future, the sort of control that was counter-intuitive to who she was. That didn't mean that there wasn't this sizzle of chemistry between them. He looked at her with brooding interest, trying to prise beneath the surface to where her thoughts were hidden.

'There's something I think you need to know, Rocco.' Ella could feel him trying to get inside her head. He'd asked whether she was tempted by his money. He couldn't begin to understand just how much of a turn-off it was because the man who was the billionaire wasn't the man who'd listened to her, laughed with her and heard all her confidences. *He* was who she'd given her heart to and that guy hadn't been bolstered by money.

'I don't know how to tell you this, but I'll start by saying that I did my best to find you. I had no idea that you hadn't wanted to be found.' Her heart picked up pace and began to beat like a sledgehammer against her ribcage.

'We agreed that what we had wouldn't last for ever,' Rocco murmured. 'You told me that I brought out an adventurous side to you and… I'll admit that being someone else brought out something in me as well. I'm honest enough to admit that. I relaxed in a way I haven't done before, but I always knew that the end would come, which was why I walked away. And I meant to keep walking until…' he grimaced '…until I found that something inside me wouldn't let me carry on. I'm not saying anything I haven't already told you.'

'You hurt me.' She hated that admission but, even now and even in these circumstances, it was just too raw to keep to herself.

'I never meant to do that. Please believe me… I was born into responsibility. My family… I've been primed to take over vast business concerns. I could spend time explaining what that means in terms of my personal relationships but, in essence, the life you want and deserve would never be one I could give you.'

'I'm glad you said that.'

'Come again?'

'I'm glad you said that because you'll know, from the start, that I don't want anything from you when I tell you that I'm pregnant.'

CHAPTER FIVE

THE SILENCE WAS DEAFENING.

'Did you hear what I just said? Rocco, I'm pregnant. That's why I tried to find you after you walked away. It wasn't because I wanted to hunt you down so that I could try and revive anything.'

Restless, and fighting another surge of anger when she thought about how she'd been played, Ella pushed herself off the sofa and walked jerkily to the sideboard to pour herself a glass of water. Then she turned round and remained where she was, staring at him, eyes narrowed with hostility.

'You ask me whether I would consider re-starting where we left off now that I know how much money you have. Is that really the person you think I am? I... The man I went to bed with wasn't *you*. The man I ended up caring about isn't the person standing in front of me asking whether I'd consider sleeping with him because he's rich!'

'Slow down, Ella. Rewind!'

'Yes, you made me feel exciting and daring and...and *free*. And you say that I made you feel more relaxed, because with me you were someone else, but that someone else was a *lie*, Rocco! Did you come back here when you didn't have to because you wanted to take a little time out from being a big shot and you figured I would buy into that because you could pay me?'

'No!'

'I didn't have to tell you about this. I could have kept it to myself. When I found out that you didn't exist... Well, what sort of man *were* you?'

'I've already explained myself, Ella. Now is the time to move away from that and... I can't believe what you've just told me. You're *pregnant*?'

'If you'd told me that you couldn't be bothered to stay here, couldn't care about the fate of all the people here—some of whom have worked in this department store for decades—then I think I really would have turned my back on you and kept this thing to myself!'

Rocco stared at her.

Pregnant? This was the last thing he'd expected in a million years. Yes, maybe he'd come back to recapture some of that weird freedom he'd felt when he'd been with her. Maybe he'd wanted to test the ground, see whether the electricity that had surged between them was still there. Had he imagined that he could influence her in some way because now she would know what he was worth? Maybe. He'd never been short of women who were impressed by his vast reserves of wealth.

Was that belief so firmly embedded in him that he had simply tarred her with the same brush without bothering to dig a little deeper? To realise that she was not at all like any of the women he had dated or slept with in the past?

He'd been a different man with her and maybe it wasn't because he'd had a new, assumed identity. He'd been a different man with her because she was a different woman.

Bit by bit, he realised that the issue of the pregnancy—which was still reverberating inside him like a bomb waiting to be fully detonated—would have to take a back seat to all her outpourings. She was carrying his baby. Not for a single moment did he not believe that fact.

She was also seething with bitterness and resentment. To get to the big thing that needed to be discussed, he would first have to find a way through her hostility.

'Say that again.'

'Which bit? The bit where I tell you that you're *nothing* like the guy I remember? The bit where I tell you that you did a good job camouflaging your *arrogance*, all the better to *seduce me*?'

'The bit where you tell me that you felt you had to put me to the test before letting me know that I'm going to be a father!'

Rocco raked his fingers through his hair and buried his head in his hands.

How? How the hell had this happened? He knew; of course he did. They'd made love like two people who had spent a lifetime starved of sex. He'd been careful but there had been times, at least two, when he had stirred in the middle of the night, reached out to feel her warm body next to him and hadn't been able to resist…

In that carefree bubble, he'd managed to make the ultimate mistake: he'd lost control. He'd spent his entire adult life reminding himself of the dangers of losing control and he'd fallen victim to the very thing he had preached about.

Playing any kind of blame game wasn't going to do, as he now faced the inescapable truth which was that every plan he'd ever made was dissolving in front of his very eyes. Blame games weren't going to work and arguing wasn't going to work.

Right now she was upset and furious with him. That was certainly the last thing he needed because the situation would have to be dealt with calmly and rationally. But he could understand where she was coming from and he wanted to hit something very hard in sheer frustration.

'Sometimes it's better for a child to just not know one parent rather than have a parent who doesn't take an interest. I was brought up in a very happy family unit. What would it have felt like if I'd thought that my dad had chosen not to have anything to do with me? If he'd known of my existence and then decided that I wasn't worth the effort? If you'd been prepared to walk away without a backward glance because you wouldn't be getting what you came here for, then you would have been that man. Maybe you still are. Maybe there *is* no Jose underneath the Rocco.'

'How the hell can you make a judgement like that?' But Rocco knew how. He'd set in chain a sequence of consequences and, whilst he knew that he wasn't to blame, he could see how she might view the situation through a different lens.

And yet, for him, there could be only one solution to the mess in which they now found themselves: marriage. The thought of any child of his being illegitimate was beyond acceptable.

'When you suddenly find that you're going to have a baby, your brain gets very sharp.'

'I can't have this conversation here, Ella.'

He moved to grab his coat, which he had slung over the back of a chair. It was black cashmere, as soft as butter.

'Would it make a difference where we have this conversation?'

'When this store opens, people will be coming and going. We'll be interrupted non-stop. We can't huddle in the corner talking about this...this...'

'Nightmare?'

'Don't put words into my mouth. What happened, happened, and resorting to sarcasm isn't going to change that. We are still where we are, and where we are demands a solution. This is a shock for me, so expect a shocked reaction.'

Dark, cool eyes collided with narrowed green ones. Ella scowled and looked away. He moved towards the door and she followed suit, first telling him that she had to fetch her coat.

'I'll meet you outside,' Rocco said. 'At this stage, maybe leaving together might raise one or two eyebrows. I don't care, but you might.'

'Sooner or later people will find out.'

'But you might appreciate the *later* option.' He held her gaze. 'You have a lot you want to say. I understand. I have quite a bit to say myself. The bridge between us will have to be crossed, even if you might think that I'm not the man you thought I was.'

Ella breathed in deeply.

He was right. Right that they were where they were,

right that being on constant attack wouldn't change anything. A bomb had detonated in the very heart of his well-ordered life and he'd somehow taken it in his stride. It didn't matter how angry she was, how much his very presence made her realise the fool she'd been. She raged that he was acting like an adult and his cool, sensible response wasn't what she wanted, because what did she want—a declaration that he'd suddenly realised that she'd meant more to him than a fleeting romp between the sheets? She'd meant nothing to him when it came to any emotional bond. He'd come back to see if they could temporarily pick up where they'd left off and she loathed that that *hurt*.

Shame at her own weakness and determination to hang onto her pride stiffened her, and she pursed her lips tightly.

'If you tell me where we're going, I can meet you there once I've fetched my coat.'

'My hotel.'

'That's the last place I'm going,' Ella said with scathing dismissal.

'What's the problem with that?'

'Because *I don't want to*. Because I would rather we have this conversation on neutral territory.'

For a few seconds Rocco didn't say anything and then he shrugged. 'Ella, the hotel is in Dublin, half an hour away by taxi. There's a very big, very comfortable breakfast area where we can continue this conversation in complete privacy.'

Ella thought about all the people she knew in the store and in town. She hadn't kept her pregnancy a secret; what would have been the point? She'd vaguely said something and nothing about an affair that hadn't worked out, somehow making it sound as though she had been having a clandestine relationship for weeks, maybe months. No one knew the identity of the father. She'd never been an open book and everyone had been respectful of her reticence. Including her father, even though she had seen the disappointment and concern on his face when she'd broken the news to him.

The horror of ever confessing that she'd had a fling with a guy who had walked away without a backward glance and, worse, had done his utmost to make sure she didn't get in touch with him, hadn't borne thinking about. Did she want to be seen with Rocco in the local café where Sheila, the town gossip, would serve them tea and then promptly relay the sighting on the local grapevine? Dublin at least guaranteed anonymity and he was right: when it came to the world finding out, the *later* option held definite appeal.

'My driver will take me there and I'll pay for you to take a taxi. We can be assured of privacy without any curious looks or conclusions being formed, because I guess everyone knows that you're pregnant.'

'Not *everyone's* in the dark. I'm four months' pregnant. It's not something I can keep to myself for ever. It's just that no one knows who the father of my baby is.'

Rocco tilted his head to the side and looked at her in silence for a few seconds. He would have to tread carefully. Perhaps, for the first time in a life in which he was accustomed to having all orders obeyed and all needs immediately met, Rocco was discovering what it felt like to run headlong into an immovable roadblock.

The very thing that had beguiled him—her lack of awe of what he could bring to the table financially—was now the very thing that stood in the way of the most logical conclusion to this situation. She'd been positively insulted at the insinuation that she might be impressed by his wealth. She couldn't be swayed by any amount of money and, whatever they'd shared, her opinion of him now couldn't be lower. She barely liked him. She had spun him the story about the fate of the staff as a way of measuring his worth just to see whether she should even bother to tell him about the pregnancy. If he'd shut down the conversation without discussion, he uneasily suspected she would have withheld the news about the pregnancy, judging him to be the sort of guy a kid is better off without.

Maybe in due course, when their child had become old enough to be curious, she might have done something about that. He'd never considered fatherhood with any immediacy but, now that it had been thrust upon him, he was very clear on what he wanted. Doing the honourable thing was top of the list. He had been raised to value duty, after all, to value the virtue of responsibility. Right now, he was skating on thin ice when it came to achieving his goal.

He couldn't fault her hostility. She had been open and trusting with him, had confided in him and, in return, she had been repaid with what she would see as colossal betrayal. Rocco knew that if he were to suggest the honourable thing—marriage for the sake of their baby—she would recoil in horror. As she'd told him, he was the last person she would ever again want to be involved with.

But he was going to marry her. That was a given. He was going to give his flesh and blood the legacy he or she deserved, the legacy that was their natural birthright.

He told her the name of the hotel where he was staying, and watched the way she lowered her eyes. What would she be thinking? That this five star hotel was the last place she would have associated with the man she'd thought he was? The guy she'd trusted?

Rocco thought of the houses, the cars, his mansion in London…of the exalted background he had so carefully hidden from her.

It was what it was and he *was* going to get what he wanted. He wasn't used to playing the long game but choices seemed thin on the ground at the moment.

'It must have been scary for you, Ella,' he murmured now, pausing by the door to look down at her with genuine sympathy. 'No, don't say anything. We can talk about all of this when we're at the hotel. I'll give you time to tell the boss that you won't be in today.'

'For a couple of hours, at any rate.'

'Let's not put a timeline on the discussion we're going to have to have. You…you don't look pregnant.'

'Don't you believe me?'

'Can you try to stop attacking me? That's not what I meant. I believe you. I wasn't as careful with protection as I should have been so, trust me, I not only believe you but I take full responsibility for…this situation.'

'I'm not blameless.' She looked at him mutinously, then lowered her eyes again. 'It's nearly four months,' she said.

'From everything I've read, you don't really show with a first pregnancy until later on.'

Rocco glanced at his watch. 'Let's say I meet you at twelve? Gives you quite some time here to do whatever urgent things you might have to do…'

'That would be dealing with the winding up of the store.'

'And we can have some lunch.'

'I…'

'Please don't tell me that you're not hungry because I've offered to buy lunch for you. You need to eat—you're pregnant. That much I do know without having read anything on the subject. Are you? Eating properly?'

'Of course I am. I'm more than capable of looking after myself.' She hesitated, then said in a semi-resentful rush, 'I've been for a scan and everything is fine with the baby.'

'Do you know…what we're having?'

Ella stared at him.

She could feel a slow burn inside her, something different from the anger, hurt and resentment. Over the months she had become accustomed to this being her baby, her situation, *her* responsibility. But now she saw that letting him in would unlock all sorts of other things. She would be opening the door to his presence in her life in ways that wouldn't be politely respectful if she decided she didn't want him to be there. He had a stake in what was going on inside her body and that scared her because she knew that she had feelings for him.

At least, for the man she'd thought she'd known. But Jose was Rocco and Rocco… For all the accusations she had thrown at him, he wasn't walking away, wasn't raging at her, wasn't blaming her for what had happened and wasn't telling her that he'd ruined his life even though he might think it.

'I don't want to know.'

'Right, I'll see you in a couple of hours, Ella.' He paused. 'And I should tell you that I won't be impressed if you decide to bail on me because you want to give me space to process. Or any other reason, for that matter.'

'Whether you're impressed by anything I do or don't do isn't my concern.'

'Listen to me. We're in this together, so you will have to be civil at some point. I can't keep explaining why I did what I did on an endless loop.'

'I know that. Can you get that it hurt when I found out that you'd lied? My ex lied to me because he wanted my flatmate, not me. Do you get that it felt like a very similar road I was walking down? And then you show up here, telling me that you're actually the guy who's bought the store… Do you get that it all feels *a little bloody overwhelming?*'

'Ella…'

'Forget it.'

She made to turn away and felt his hand circle her wrist, tugging her slightly towards him.

'It matters,' Rocco said gruffly. 'Believe it or not, I'm not that guy. I don't lie. Ever. What I did… Yes, I wasn't straight with you, but I really never meant to get involved and, once I had, I couldn't then tell you what was going on. I'm sorry.'

'Okay.' Ella pulled back but her heart was hammering

and she could feel herself weakening at the sincerity in his voice and the gravity of his expression.

She wasn't going to weaken. He might be sincere but, even so, he could never be her type: a billionaire who could have his pick of women, who lived life in the fast lane, who had basically dallied with her for a bit of fun because of a passing attraction. Besides, whatever he said about being unable to be honest with her, he could have been. Everyone in life had a choice.

'Is it? Okay?'

'It's okay insofar as you're right,' Ella said coolly. 'We need to be civil with one another. Basically, what we had was more or less a one-night stand between two people who aren't compatible, who come from completely different worlds. I'll try to forget the past and just think about what happens next in this scenario.'

'We weren't *that* incompatible.'

'We were good in bed,' Ella said flatly. 'So, sure, in that sense we weren't incompatible, but I don't go for rich, powerful guys who go through life knowing that they can do exactly what they want.'

'Right. This rich guy will see you at midday.'

On the Tannoy system, Christmas music burst into life, tinny and joyful, and Rocco involuntarily grimaced. 'It's at least the season for goodwill,' he said. He waited a couple of seconds, got nothing by way of response, then he spun round, half-turned to give her a small salute and was gone, closing the door to the boardroom quietly behind him.

Ella stared at the closed door until the tangle of emotions racing through her began to settle.

Over the months, she'd been lulled into believing that she was going to have to make the best of her circumstances. She would be a single parent, would struggle to make ends meet but would have the love and support of her dad and her friends. She was grateful for living in a small, close-knit community.

Now, walking into that boardroom, seeing the man who had haunted her waking moments and her deepest dreams, sitting there... Even thinking about it made her shiver with a sense of unreality. She'd fainted. Something she'd never done before in her life. The shock... In a single instant, the life she'd come to terms with had been turned on its head.

She did a few things that couldn't wait, made some lame excuses to her colleagues, Vera and her boss and then, at exactly a quarter to twelve, she got a cab to the city centre.

The season of goodwill was in full swing outside the department store. The Christmas lights were on and the store fronts were bursting with giant bows and bunches of poppy-red holly. Outside Maccie's, the local butcher, a blow-up Santa bobbed, along with three reindeer. Over the past few days, the snow had been obliging when it came to creating just the right atmosphere and it was lightly falling now, as though dusting everything with icing sugar.

She felt furtive as she climbed into a taxi from the rank outside the one and only hotel in the town. She had time to think as the taxi purred towards Dublin centre. Did it help? Did it calm her? Nothing could stop the steady spiral of bewilderment and confusion that underplayed the biting disappointment, hurt and the sinking feeling that she had made the same mistake all over again.

They approached the city and the explosion of festive lights took her breath away. A giant Christmas tree dominated the square outside an enormous store, decorated with over-sized ornaments in shades of red, green and gold. People were everywhere, scurrying like ants, clutching bags and heavily bundled up in coats and scarves, their breath visible in the cold winter air as they breathed out. Light flurries of snow barely collected on the glistening pavements. There was a Christmas market on and she could smell the spiced aroma of mulled wine and mince pies.

Her stomach clenched with sudden tension as the taxi slowed in front of the hotel. Outside the lights were delicate, gossamer-thin lacy webs stretching elegantly across the façade. Two liveried men stood on either side of imposing glass doors and sprang into action as soon as she approached.

She breathed in sharply when she spotted Rocco sitting on one of the sofas at the back of the room. The gorgeous, lavish decorations, the elegant tree discreetly positioned by the bar, the massive vases stuffed with poinsettias, chrysanthemums and amaryllis all faded as her mouth went dry and her heart began to pound.

Jose and Rocco merged into one man, sinfully sexy... and breathtakingly beautiful.

She walked briskly towards him and it was only when she was standing in front of him that he looked up from what he was doing on his phone and stood to greet her.

'Ella.'

Rocco had sensed her but only looked up when she cast a shadow over him. Sprawled on the sofa, he'd sucked in a sharp breath as their eyes had tangled, and for a few seconds he'd been catapulted back to when they'd been lovers. To that taste of freedom, releasing part of him that had been completely authentic. He was too level-headed to be seduced into thinking that could have lasted for ever but it had still lodged inside him like a burr.

He'd gone past the shock. As he'd waited for her, his brain had begun to whirr along more practical lines. The end objective remained the same: marriage. With that in mind, he would feel out the lay of the land and, if she dug in her heels, then he would persuade her in whatever other ways it took. Getting lost in what had happened would have to be put on ice because where would it get either of them?

He had to break through her disillusionment. He would be businesslike in his approach. His views on marriage, on love, on the relevance of emotions, were so deeply ingrained that when he thought about marrying her it was exclusively on a no choice basis. He wasn't a man who fled in the face of responsibility. They'd had fun but she had never been on his radar for anything long term. Now that he was going to be in it for the long haul—even though she didn't know that yet—he felt it was important that he first got her on side and, second, clarified the parameters.

He would be a loyal husband and a dutiful father. He knew the value of responsibility. His uncle had set a terrible example of how to waste a life away. No flights of fancy or self-delusion for Rocco. As cold a parent as he was, his father had done what had to be done when it came to taking the mess his brother had left behind and dealing with it. He had been able to do that because he'd had the right woman by his side. A woman there through arrangement rather than love, brought up in a family in which duty also came first, who had allowed him the time to devote to work. Rocco could scarcely recall his father being around when he'd been growing up. Nor could he recall his equally cool mother ever complaining.

'A woman who's demanding is a woman who will drag you down. Look at your uncle. He liked women who wanted his undivided attention; it made him feel wanted. He was a weak man. Pay attention to where that got him.'

Rocco wouldn't pretend that there would be wild flights of love…although there would certainly be passion. Just thinking about touching her sent him into instant arousal. So, no problems on that front. It would be a better outcome than the icy coldness of his parents' marriage, even if it could never be what she might want. She thought he was a liar, which was an appellation he found distasteful, but he couldn't blame her.

As she sat down and faced him, Rocco tried to glean what she was thinking, but the green eyes staring back at him were veiled.

'Are you hungry?' he asked. 'I can order something for us to eat now or we can talk a bit first and eat afterwards.'

'I'll have some mince pies to start with.'

'Mince pies. Would you call that *food*?'

'My tastes have changed. I crave them.'

He ordered the mince pies and was amused at how enthusiastically she tucked into them when they came.

'You're hungry.'

'Only for mince pies right now. Aren't you going to have one?'

'Not my thing. I've had time to think,' he said seriously. 'It goes without saying that my preferred option here would be for us to marry.'

Ella's eyebrows shot up but, before she could push back at that, he smoothly continued. 'But, as you've already told me, I'm the last person you would go for.'

'Yes, because what I want is love. That's the glue that keeps a family bonded. I don't want someone to tell me that they'll put a ring on my finger because together we've made a mistake and now there's a baby on the way! Do you think I've lived my life dreaming of the day when I might become someone's burden? My parents had a wonderful, supportive, loving marriage and that's something I've dreamt of for myself. I see my brother in love with the woman he married, companions and best friends, there for one another. Now you tell me that marriage is the *preferred option* here! Well, that just sends a shiver of joy through me! I'm guessing you wouldn't even be sitting here if it weren't for the fact that you had to do your duty!'

'I don't *have* to do anything, Ella. I *choose* to be here—and, just for the record, *duty* isn't a dirty word.'

'And love? Does that get a look in?'

'Love isn't a sentiment I recognise.'

'That's awful.'

'I'm thinking about what would be best for our baby. If you find the thought of marriage to me unacceptable, then let's discuss the practicalities. Where are you living at the moment?'

'Currently with my dad, but naturally that won't be an ongoing situation. And I happen to be thinking about *our baby* as well, Rocco! A loveless marriage does nothing when it comes to providing what a child needs.'

'You've made your case, Ella. You don't have to drive the point home. Back to your living arrangements. I'll be buying you a house.'

'Hold on just a minute! Don't think you can swan in here and start telling me what I can and can't do!'

'No, Ella, *you* hold on. I didn't see this coming and neither did you. You might think it's acceptable for your pride to be in the driving seat, because what you'd really like is the fairy tale dream of happy-ever-after in a situation like this, but there's no room for pride here and you'd better start accepting that.'

'Or else what?'

'Or else I can safely say that your concerns revolve around yourself and have nothing to do with this baby, whatever you say to the contrary. I won't be able to relocate here, but I will buy a house close by for weekend use. This isn't about telling you what you can and can't do. This is about practicalities. I'm rich and I can afford it.'

'Where do you even live?' Ella suddenly asked 'Spain? Not Ireland, I'm sure. Isn't it going to be inconvenient for you traipsing up here all the time?'

'I have bases in a number of countries, and nothing's inconvenient when you have a private jet at your disposal. At any rate, I can personally oversee work on the store and remote work as needs be.'

'Private jet…'

'Additionally, I will set up an account for you. You'll

find that you'll have more than enough money to do whatever you want.'

'An account for *the baby*,' Ella corrected.

Rocco ignored that. With his end goal in sight, he intended to hammer home all the advantages that would come with being his wife. 'Of course, should you meet someone else, then...' He eloquently shrugged his shoulders and sat back, allowing her to register that possibility.

Out of the corner of his eye, he noted her taking stock of something she hadn't thought about.

'By which,' he hammered home, 'I mean some renegotiation would have to take place. I won't be paying for another guy's upkeep.'

'*Another guy's upkeep?* It's months before I even *have* the baby. At what point will this *other guy* come along, demanding to *be kept*? This is all moving way too fast!'

'I'm not a man who likes to take chances,' he said smoothly. 'You could say this is the outcome of taking a chance, or at any rate of losing sight of self-control. You ask when some guy might come along looking to be kept? You're going to be a very wealthy woman. You'll be surprised at how many men will start circling because of your money.'

'I really don't think we need to—'

'And naturally, there's me, while we're discussing probable scenarios.'

'I beg your pardon?'

'I would want a wife, and sooner rather than later. But, you're right, let's not get ahead of ourselves.' He waved that aside dismissively, shrewd enough to know that the idea would find a way into her head. 'To be discussed at a later date, no doubt. First on the agenda will be accommodation that's suitable for us and, after that, we can work on the details of finances and the rest. I'm assuming, at least for now, that lawyers need not be involved?'

'No!'

'Good.' Rocco nodded. 'Like it or not, we're in this together, Ella, so stop fighting me. Let's enjoy lunch and we can talk about…whatever you think needs doing at the department store as a final hurrah. And one more thing?'

'What's that? I don't think I'm up to dealing with much more at the moment.'

'Your father? I would like to meet him, and today seems as good a day as any to do that.'

CHAPTER SIX

A WIFE? SOONER rather than later?

What happened to the marriage proposal? He'd certainly accepted her refusal at the speed of light!

The bill was paid and as Ella was faffing, gathering her gloves and idly checking her phone for messages. She said casually, 'You would want a wife sooner rather than later, you say?'

She started sticking on the gloves and surreptitiously stared at Rocco from under her lashes. He didn't believe in love, and didn't think it was necessary for a healthy, happy marriage, so of course he wouldn't have a problem marrying a woman just to be a mother to their child, to provide the family unit he thought was important. A woman who would probably come from the same background as him. A rich, beautiful socialite who wouldn't make a nuisance of herself by demanding shows of love and affection.

She felt a dizzying tightness in her chest at the thought of that. It was fine waving aside a marriage proposal as unacceptable because it didn't meet her requirements. It was a little different when the marriage proposal was then airbrushed out of existence to give way to the possibility of another woman stepping in to fill the space.

'You have a problem with that?'

'I just think it's a bit early in the day to be putting it on the table.'

'Why?'

'Because...' She looked at him with consternation, hardly aware that he was wrapping her scarf round her neck and handing her the woolly hat that she had dumped on the table. She absently stuck it on and continued to gaze at him as she formulated something that resembled a reasonable explanation as to why she was so bothered at the thought of him with another woman.

'I believe that a child needs to have the benefit of a mother and a father.'

'So do I.'

'Ah, but key difference here—I won't be on an endless quest to find a suitable partner I'm in love with who can fit the bill. I don't believe that love is the be all and end all. In fact, when I think about it...' he slotted her arm into the crook of his and began ushering her out of the restaurant '...if you look at the divorce rate between people who declare undying love on their wedding day, only to relegate that to undying indifference or everlasting resentment a decade later, well, the statistics say it all.

'My driver is waiting. I think I'll get rid of him so we can drive together to your house and I can meet your father.'

'My parents were blissfully happy.'

'That's called the exception to the rule.'

'Your parents...?'

'Still together.'

'Which just shows...'

'Ella.' Rocco stopped and looked down at her, breaking contact and shoving his hands in the pockets of his coat. 'My parents' marriage was a business deal that brought together two important houses. They stayed together because they both understood how the world they inherited worked. They knew the rules.'

'You say stuff like that, Rocco, and I'm talking to a complete stranger.'

'Only when it comes to the details of my life,' Rocco said gruffly. 'One thing I do know is that, yes, I would want a wife by my side with a child in the equation.' He paused, giving her time to digest the scenario he was painting for her.

'A wife who comes from the same class as you? *Knows the rules*, like your mother did?'

'Preferably a wife who is the mother of my child but, failing that, then yes, quite possibly.'

Ella's mouth went dry. She felt jealousy, and she didn't know where that was coming from, because surely she should hate him? Hadn't he lied to her? Why would you be jealous of someone who'd lied to you, someone you justifiably hated? Yet if there was hatred there then it was well and truly swamped by the steady thump of possessiveness that coursed through her. Besides, the way he was now—the man willing to accept a situation he could never have banked on; the guy who still had that flare of fairness and consideration inside him—was no convenient cardboard cutout, easy for her to dismiss...

'I... I don't know anything about your parents. How

do you think they'll react?' This to sidestep the rush of emotion inside her.

'That's something I haven't yet considered. I'm still in the process of trying to come to terms with the situation myself. Don't forget you've had a head start on me.'

'Not my fault I couldn't locate you!' This felt safer, and she broke eye contact, but her heart was still thudding as she clocked the sleek, black Range Rover idling on the other side of the road.

Rocco thought it best to steer her away from picking back up that line of attack. He'd given her food for thought. It was clear she didn't approve of the thought of another woman stepping into his life, and she certainly had a point when she'd said that it was a bit early to paint a future that involved other partners, but all was fair in love and war.

He wondered whether she was *jealous*, and then was surprised at the kick that gave him. The thought of her with another man didn't sit well with him. Was that jealousy or was it just that he was the sort of guy who could never like the thought of another man adopting a fatherly role to his offspring? He'd never had a jealous bone in his body but when he thought of Ella in the arms of someone else…

'Do you want to give your father some warning that I'll be coming along?'

'Maybe this isn't a good idea.'

'It's a very good idea.' He dismissed his driver and helped her into the passenger seat but held open the door, maintaining his calm. As far as Rocco was concerned, there were still a million practicalities to pin down, but he would let those wait for the time being.

A place for her to live? He would bide his time.

A car of her choice? In due course.

The details of maintenance? A bridge to be crossed.

At the back of his mind was the thought that those things would not have to be seriously addressed because she would come to him before that. She would recognise the advantages of marriage and would accept that sometimes flights of fancy when it came to fairy stories of love and romance get put to bed in the face of duties and responsibilities that would always take precedence. He would drop the subject of marriage and just let time do its thing.

'You're nervous about me meeting your father. Why? Is it because you told yourself that this situation would never arise? Because I was never going to show up in your life again?'

'Something like that.'

'And, now that I've shown up, you're nervous because…?'

'I'm not sure how my father is going to react to you,' Ella said bluntly.

'He's not going to think I'm a catch?' Rocco raised his eyebrows and grinned. 'Steady employment…good sense of responsibility…happy to put out the bins on a Monday…'

He watched pink creep into her cheeks and was gratified when she smiled at him, relaxing for the first time since he'd surprised her in the boardroom. This was the Ella he'd left in his wake and, if he could have turned back the hands of time, maybe he wouldn't have been so hasty in his departure.

It wasn't as though leaving that bubble behind had been a roaring success. He hadn't been able to relegate her to something fun that had happened one day. She'd preyed on his mind, which was why he had finally made his way back to her. Back to her and, vaguely, back to try and recapture something of that carefree man who had had a window in time during which he had broken free of what had always been expected of him.

Everything that subsequently happened had come as a shock. But to see her smile that sweet, hesitant smile suddenly made him feel ten feet tall.

'When I began looking for you, I was looking for an ordinary guy,' she said truthfully. 'Someone I could relate to. Someone who shared the same worries and concerns that I did.'

'Tell me I'm not sharing the same worries and concerns right now that you're facing,' Rocco said.

The snow flurries pricked his face like needles. It was freezing, but no way was he going to abandon this conversation, because right now she wasn't attacking him and he was going to take that as a win of sorts. He understood her bitterness but he was determined to find a way through that because he had to. There was no choice.

'It's cold. You should get in the car.'

'I'm a big boy. I can withstand a little cold weather. Besides, I don't want you to clam up on me.'

'I'm not going to clam up on you.'

'And I don't want you to return to the comfort zone of attacking me for what happened. I want you to tell me what to expect when I meet your father. Will I be greeted with a shotgun and a pack of rabid dogs? What have you said to him?'

'I'm not talking to you until you're in the car. If you end up catching pneumonia, then I'll probably feel guilty, and you wouldn't deserve my guilt.'

'That's reasonable.'

He skirted around into the driver's seat and slammed the door behind him. He swivelled in his seat, leant against the door and looked at her in silence.

It was a feat of willpower for Ella to hold that dark, steady, unrevealing gaze and she half-wished she'd let him stand outside the car, shivering in the cold.

'Okay.' She sighed. 'My dad isn't going to know what to do with you. He's a straightforward guy and I don't think he's met anyone like you in his life before. Not only are you the guy who gets his daughter pregnant, but Rocco, you...you're...'

'Spit it out, Ella.'

'You're *from another planet*.'

'The money thing?'

'Yes, *the money thing*.'

'I never thought you were a snob.'

'Don't be ridiculous. I'm anything but a snob! I happen to have grown up in a very normal household. My dad has a small farm, my mum worked at Hailey's for years. How can I be a snob?'

'Aren't you pigeonholing me because of my background? Isn't that the definition of being a snob?'

'No.' But she flushed.

'Take the money out of the equation and I'm the same man you slept with three months ago.'

Ella opened her mouth to contradict him but she hesitated because, whilst she had initially been utterly unable to equate Jose with Rocco, the lines were becoming blurred. She had seen him in that boardroom and shock had catapulted her into a reaction that had been fast, spontaneous and unforgiving.

And then his outward sophistication—the expensive suit, the hand-made shoes, the priceless watch—meant he was no more the laid-back, charming guy but a cool, self-assured man with the confidence of someone accustomed to being obeyed.

Yet hadn't he been self-assured when she'd first met him? He'd strolled into her office and looked around him as though he owned the place.

'Not quite.'

'So I'm not what he's expecting on a number of fronts. What, exactly, have you told him about me?'

'I haven't said much...'

'Your idea of not saying much and my idea of not saying much are probably at opposite ends of the scale,' Rocco said truthfully.

'Maybe.'

Rocco slid a sideways glance at her. Outside, leaden, yellow sky was gathering snow. Christmas was all around them, in the lights everywhere and the excitement of shoppers stocking up.

He started the engine, the powerful motor roared into life then he edged out of the parking space.

'Can I say something, Ella?'

'You've already said quite a lot.'

'You must have been distraught when you couldn't locate me, when you realised that I'd given you a false name, but you were strong, and you still are, and I admire that. Whatever road this takes us, you can be guaranteed, always and for ever, of my complete support.'

For her, what had happened was as huge and as life-changing as it was for him, and she had dealt with it admirably even when she'd assumed that she'd be dealing with it on her own. Through all of that, she'd still had it in her to be concerned for the store that would for ever change the face of the town when it was converted into flats and offices.

'Do you get why the offices and apartments are going to work for the town? I'm going to be sticking around to answer any questions the staff might have, but I'd like to find out what exactly your thoughts are, bearing in mind that you're sentimentally attached to the place.'

'I was upset when the news first broke but…okay, yes. And I appreciate what you're doing…with trying to keep everything as sustainable as possible.'

'Think we might be making headway in breaking down some of the barriers between us?'

Ella shrugged.

'Because it's important, as we're going to be in one another's lives for a very long time, in one way or another.'

'One way or another?'

'Be it if I marry or if you do…'

Ella's lips thinned as she was forced to confront once again the idea that he would find someone else. She hated the thought of it. She wanted to ask him what his parents might think of her and then wondered whether he would even bother introducing her to them if she wasn't actively involved in his life. What would be the point? They probably lived in Spain. That would be where the family business was. A haughty, aristocratic couple, parents of a treasured only son who would meet a haughty, aristocratic wife who would be the sort of woman he would choose to marry.

Her imagination refused to be reined in. She feverishly imagined her child in this scenario and went cold inside. Having earlier scoffed at him for introducing a layer of complication that wasn't necessary because their baby hadn't even been born, Ella now found herself dwelling on all manner of unpleasant scenarios that somehow involved her being sidelined as a parent in the years to come.

She snapped back to the present. He'd programmed her address into the satnav but the going was slow because of the weather.

'So...'

His lazy drawl made her half-turn so that she could look at his sharp, aristocratic profile.

'You were going to give me the low down on what your father might be expecting.'

'Okay.' She sighed. 'I may have said that I had feelings for you.'

'Come again?'

'You heard me.'

'I think I need to hear you again so I can process what you said.'

'You don't actually have to hear it again to process anything because you can leave all the talking to me. You'll find out soon enough that my dad isn't very communicative. He'll really only feel comfortable talking to me, so you can take a back seat and go with the flow.'

'I'm not sure that works for me. No, I *know* that doesn't work for me. When you say you had feelings for me…?'

'I don't have feelings for you! I had to say something!' Ella shot him an exasperated sigh.

Everything was suddenly so complicated. Was he being deliberately obtuse? Couldn't he just accept what she was telling him and let her get on with it?

No, he couldn't. That wasn't his nature, and besides, he wasn't being obtuse. He was genuinely curious because, looked at through dispassionate, objective eyes, why wouldn't she simply have come out with the truth— that she'd had a quick fling and a mistake had been the unfortunate result?

'No one asked for lengthy explanations, if you really want to know. I've never been one to confide, as you well know, but I also would never normally hop into bed with some passing stranger. And when it comes to my dad, well, he knows me better than anyone, and I didn't want to break his heart even more than it was breaking already, so I said I'd fallen for a guy but the relationship hadn't worked out.'

'Because the guy had lied about who he was?'

'Because the guy and I decided it just wouldn't have been the right thing.'

'And the reason I stayed away for nearly four months?'

'I just said I had to come to terms with everything before… I involved someone who wouldn't have welcomed involvement. And, now that I've explained this to you, will you please trust me and let me do the talking?'

'What is this conversation going to look like? Can you give me a sample taster so I know what to expect?'

'The left turn to the farm's coming up, but you have to go really slowly or you'll miss it.'

'Well?'

'I don't know. I'll play it by ear.'

'I see.'

Ella looked at him narrowly because she had no idea what was going through Rocco's head. She'd said precious little about Rocco because, at the time, she'd known precious little about him aside from the fact that he'd appeared in her life and then vanished without trace, thereby proving himself to be just the sort of guy she should never have gone near.

Confessing to her beloved, quiet dad that she'd had a two-week liaison with a man who had never wanted any sort of relationship with her would have left him confused and saddened. So she'd told him that she'd lost her heart to a wonderful man and that they had parted company on the best of terms because they'd reached the same conclusion: that the relationship wouldn't work out.

And she had left it there. For the time being. Now, though…

The house appeared, emerging from the gathering gloom and the drizzle of snow, a two-storied building squatting in the middle of acres of land. The lights were on downstairs and she knew what she would find when she went in. Her father settled in the sitting room with the fire burning after a long day spent outside. There would be the smell of food cooking. He enjoyed cooking. He always had. He said it was relaxing after the gruelling physicality of tending to the land.

The car swung round in a perfect circle in front of the house and ground to a halt. When he'd killed the engine, Rocco turned to face her.

'I don't exactly know the details of what you told your father,' he said firmly. 'But the narrative from here on in will not be one in which I take a back seat. So go ahead and lead the conversation but I'm warning you to expect interruptions if I think it's going down that road.'

'How did I never notice how much you enjoy giving orders?'

But she minded less than she expected. In an uncertain place, was she somehow secretly relieved that someone was taking charge? What had happened to her feminist streak? When she thought of the reassurances he had given her earlier, she felt warm inside. When she thought about his strength, and the calm solidity of his presence, she imagined the marriage she had absolutely ruled out. Would it really be the hell on earth she had conjured up? He was a guy who had a strong moral compass and sense of responsibility. A guy who hadn't set out deliberately to lie to her but had found himself in a place where admitting the truth had not been feasible.

'I'll go inside ahead of you. My dad will have a heart attack if I produce you from out of the blue, like a rabbit from a hat.'

'Don't worry,' Rocco said after a pause. 'It's going to be fine.'

'Really?'

'Look at it this way—you were going it solo and now you're not. If not for you, then for our baby, this is surely the best possible outcome?'

In the darkness of the car, Ella could make out the glitter of his dark eyes and she felt that thread of urgent, physical awareness wash over her, waking her up to the uncomfortable recognition of a desire that had not left her in the way she had hoped it might.

And beyond desire…something deeper and far more dangerous.

'I'll come out as soon as I can,' she said shortly. 'In the meantime, please just stay here.'

'Sure. Just as long as your interpretation of *as soon as* doesn't prove to be too long.' He half-smiled. 'We're in this together now, Ella. So, like I said, don't look so anxious. When faced with a problem, two will always be better than one at dealing with it.'

Ella's heart thudded, then he reached out and trailed the back of his hand against her cheek and she felt a tide of shameless response wash through her. It was almost too much to turn away and not keen towards that warm hand and lose herself in its comforting touch.

She exited the car at speed and then took a deep breath before she inserted her key into the lock and let herself through the front door.

Rocco watched as she vanished through the door and shut it firmly behind her. Around him, the snow continued to fall gently, insistently. Away from the glittering Christmas lights strung from lamp post to lamp post in the town, out here felt quiet and remote. The house was a stone structure, sprawling in a U-shape that enfolded the courtyard where he was parked. Around it, open fields stretched through the gathering twilight in magnificent isolation.

Comfort zones had long been left behind. He was dealing with a situation for which nothing had prepared him but in truth, looking back, he felt that comfort zones had been dumped the minute he had met her. It was a relief that her explanations to her father had been perfunctory. That said, facing her father was something he would be able to deal with. *She* was the one who made his stomach twist with nerves because he didn't know where he stood with her. Because, for the first time in his life, getting what he wanted wasn't going to be a straightforward exercise and the stakes were the highest he could ever have imagined. His parents would have to be told immediately and there could be no question that he wouldn't marry the mother of his child.

He was absently staring at the door when it opened and there she was, framed in the doorway. For a few seconds, the breath was sucked out of him. She was so small, so slender, and yet right now she was singularly the most powerful person in his world.

He leapt out of the car and strode towards her. 'Ready?' he murmured, looking down at her.

She flashed him a look that was a mixture of defiance and anxiety and he recalled the sensation of her soft skin under his fingers when he had touched her cheek. The surge of physical awareness that had jolted through him.

He also recalled the fleeting but powerful acknowledgement that she had responded to that touch in a way she might not have found entirely unwelcome. He'd felt her body come alive, just for a moment, had felt the sudden softness in her and had known, on some level, that she wanted him. Desire was a difficult beast to control.

He looked at her with lazy speculation.

'Just don't say much. I've told him that you got in touch and…'

'And? Since he's under the impression that you're crazy about me, are we on course for a grand, romantic reunion?'

'No.'

'Why not?'

'Because anything between us is over and done with. You know why. I don't have to keep going into it.'

'So the part I play is…?'

'We're friends.'

'Lovers to friends,' Rocco mused. 'I always thought it went in the opposite direction—friends to lovers.'

'Not this time.'

She uneasily remembered what she had told her father—that she'd fallen for a guy before acknowledging that they lived in different worlds, worlds that would never be destined to meet. She hoped nothing she had said would come back to bite her. Fortunately for her, her dad wasn't the sort to launch into animated conversation about anything. He would eye Rocco suspiciously, would be tight-lipped and unwelcoming and she would lead the way in dispelling any notion that Rocco was anything but someone who would have no place in her future aside from fulfilling the duties of fatherhood. All Rocco had to do was go along with everything she said and keep contributions to the conversation to a minimum.

She could only hope that he wouldn't be a wild card.

As Rocco looked around him with curious eyes, what he saw was an old house, unrenovated but sturdy, built of concrete and stone, with thick walls and furnishings that were old and tired. Scott Campbell, weathered from a life spent outdoors, was proud and silent, in his mid-sixties at most, who looked much older than his years.

Rocco liked him on sight. He could deal with this man. He would enjoy it, in fact.

His handshake, as he was introduced, matched his host's in firmness. He smiled a warm, engaging, encouraging smile. At the same time, he paid utterly no attention to Ella's slight body suddenly stiffening by his side.

'Mr Campbell. I can't tell you how honoured I am to meet you and how pleased.' He lowered his voice and bent the few inches that brought him face to face with the bright blue, narrowed eyes focused on him. By the end of the evening, he intended to wipe out every scrap of wariness and suspicion. He might be cast in the role of lover turned friend but, by hook or by crook, the distinction would soon become pleasantly blurry.

He clasped the leathery hand warmly between both of his and smiled. 'Circumstances may have taken me away prematurely from your enchanting daughter, sir, but I assure you that I will not fail when it comes to fulfilling my duties supporting her in these...unexpected but very happy times...'

He sensed rather than saw the wiry body relax. Not much, but enough to encourage him. 'But I'm sure there will be ample time to discuss everything with you on that subject, to reassure you that your daughter will be supported one hundred percent by me. In the meantime... I've always had an interest in farming. I would consider myself privileged to hear everything about your farm. Who knows?' He chuckled. 'I might find there's a farmer lurking inside me somewhere...'

Rocco was invited to stay the night. Separate rooms, of course, as they were now just *friends*, but still...

Several hours later, Ella was still reeling from Rocco's charm offensive. He'd laid it on thick. Her taciturn father, known to happily spend an evening without uttering much more than a couple of sentences, had been downright loquacious.

Did Rocco actually know anything about farm equipment? Differences between agricultural tractors and regular tractors? What fertilizers were best for different crops? Weather patterns and harvesting? It seemed that he did and, what he didn't, he'd been keen to find out with the sort of phoney zeal that made her head spin.

He'd politely refused the offer of a bed but not until her father had been one hundred percent won over. When she'd made the mistake of yawning, her father had actually told her that she should go get some rest and that he'd see Rocco out!

On the spur of the moment, Ella dialled the mobile number that she now had, the very number she had previously been denied when she'd been the disposable woman he'd had a fling with.

'What do you think you're playing at?'

'Ella?'

'Of course it's me! Who else is it going to be? Do you

have women ringing you all hours? And what were you doing earlier? Didn't I tell you to leave all the talking to me?'

Dressed in thick flannel pyjamas she'd had since she'd been a teenager, Ella slid off the bed, scowling, and strolled towards the chair by the window. When she parted the curtains, she peered out into a dark wilderness with a light dusting of snow covering the fields that stretched out into infinity. Christmas was everywhere... except here. It hadn't really been here since her mother had died, even though some effort had been made for the past two Christmases. The back should have been ablaze with lights, and downstairs the tree should have been up and the stockings hung.

She let the curtain drop and tucked her knees up to her chest.

'I don't encourage women to ring me all hours, now that you mention it, and definitely not now that I'm a taken man.'

'You're not *a taken man*. I told you not to do any talking.'

'I really like your father. Clever man. We had an informative chat after you left about how he could think of diversifying to make the most of his land. Apologies if I didn't use the playbook you laid out.'

'You're not sorry at all.'

'You're right. I'm beginning to admire how well you read me.'

'As long as you left it with us just being friends.'

'As opposed to what?'

'As opposed to...to...'

'I won't lie when I tell you that marriage is the best option for us, Ella. Especially meeting your father… Family life on both sides, although it's fair to say my experience of family is wildly different to yours. He misses your mother.'

It took a couple of seconds for Ella to register the change of topic.

'Sorry?'

'Louise—your mother. He misses her every day. Especially at this time of year.'

'What are you talking about? Did he tell you that?'

'He did. Just before I left.'

Ella didn't say anything. Her father had never shared his sorrow with her after her mother had died so suddenly. He had been stalwart and silent and she hadn't quite known how to break through that barrier of quiet stoicism.

'What…what did he say?' she asked eventually. 'He… he never talked to me about that. He was there for me but I was never sure if I was ever there for him in the same way.'

Rocco's voice was a thoughtful murmur. 'I think he's a very protective dad. He didn't want to burden you with his own feelings at such a sad time. He's a strong, silent man who is perhaps a little hesitant when it comes to freely expressing emotion.'

Ella's voice was ragged and distressed. 'It's a little upsetting to think that he shared stuff with you he felt he couldn't share with me.'

'Ella, you really mustn't think that way. You must think that you're very lucky to have a father who loves you so much and whose driving desire is to always do what he thinks is best for you.'

'Thanks for saying that, Rocco,' she said gruffly, because his words helped that sudden, jarring unhappiness.

'It's the truth. He said that this Christmas is going to be very different, special, because of...our situation. I got the feeling that this baby on the way has struck him deeply.'

'Yes, I think so.'

'Which is why I'll be round first thing tomorrow morning.'

'Sorry?'

'He feels that this Christmas he would like to celebrate with a real tree instead of the silver make-do one you've used since your mother died—and maybe a party.'

'What?'

'New beginnings and all that.'

'Rocco, you weren't supposed to be talking about *new beginnings and all that*.'

'The subject of how life will change with a baby was going to arise and I had no intention of hiding from it. At any rate, like I said, I like your father. I like the fact that he doesn't talk much, but what he says is worth hearing. Makes a change from most of the population. So, if a request for a Christmas tree was made, then I'm not going to suddenly play coy and tell him that I'm not interested, because we're supposed to be just good friends, and as such my role is to hide in a cupboard of your choosing when you point to it. So the upshot is, I'll be back first thing tomorrow morning and we can go and choose a tree.'

'Wait, don't you hate Christmas?'

'"Hate" is a strong word.'

'But you're willing to go tree hunting for my dad?'

'I'm not the ogre you think I am and more than that…'

She heard the smile in his voice but the undertone remained deadly serious. 'What…?'

'More than that, I'm willing to go beyond the extra mile because this is a situation that demands it. Think about that, Ella. Can you say the same for yourself?'

CHAPTER SEVEN

'Have you forgiven me?'

Leaning against the doorframe, Rocco looked at Ella as the front door was pulled open and she shuffled her way out into the cold.

'More to the point, don't I get a cup of coffee?'

'I thought it best that we get the tree-buying done and dusted. Dad's out inspecting some fences...and forgive you for what?'

Ella had been up since six. She'd made her dad his usual pot of coffee and inwardly winced when he'd said, in his usual direct, vaguely sheepish way, 'Liked the man.'

'He's...er...' She'd struggled to find the right words to talk about friendship and reliability whilst avoiding the thorny issue of what happened next. 'A nice guy.'

'Guess that's why you fell in love with him.' Her father had looked at her in silence, his flask of coffee in one hand.

'About that, Dad...'

'Good men are hard to find. The man seems a good one to me.'

So much for her down-to-earth father having no time for a richer-than-rich billionaire, Ella had thought. Instead, she had realised uncomfortably, he had managed to do the one thing she was finding so difficult to do—he had accepted Rocco Mancini for the man he was instead of judging him because he was attached to a big bank balance.

The truth was that Rocco's parting shot had given her food for thought. He was prepared to go the extra mile. Buying a Christmas tree might be a small thing but what it represented was much bigger—a willingness to put himself out because the situation demanded it, as he'd said.

He'd asked her to marry him. She'd immediately seen that as unacceptable, because it clashed with the dreams and hopes she'd had for herself of being in a relationship where she was treasured and loved. She had made it all about her, but there was a baby inside her that they shared and, tough though it was to admit it, wasn't her immediate refusal of that marriage offer tied up with the fact that he didn't love her the way she knew, deep down, she loved him?

That was the sobering thought that had kept her awake for a lot of the night. She could rant and rave about Rocco not being the man she had given her heart to—and for sure, when she had first set eyes on him, the sophisticated billionaire with the cool, self-assured attitude hadn't matched the easy-going charmer she remembered—but now... The qualities she'd fallen for were still there.

'Penny for them.'

'Sorry?'

'Your thoughts. You're a million miles away.'

'Sorry.' She shut the door firmly behind her, pushed

it to make sure it was properly closed and then half-ran against the persisting snow to the black Range Rover.

'Forgive you for what?' was the first thing she asked as soon as Rocco was in the car, starting the engine.

'For not obeying orders yesterday.'

Ella sighed. 'You got along with my dad when I didn't think you would. I thought I could control the situation but maybe that was just wishful thinking. Everything's a muddle, and I thought it would be slightly less complicated if we kept a dividing line between you and my dad.'

She sat back and watched the dull, grey winter landscape go by as he manoeuvred the car away from the house and into the narrow lanes, taking it very, very slowly. She didn't expect him to reach out and give her hand a reassuring squeeze.

She slid her glance sideways to see that he was staring ahead, focusing on the road. When he returned his hand to the steering wheel, her heart thumped, and she still wanted those warm fingers to be clasped with hers, steady and reassuring, smoothing away all the turmoil in her head.

'He likes you,' she added.

'And that's not a good thing?'

'I suppose it's...okay.'

Rocco burst out laughing and when he cast a dark glance in her direction, she blushed, taken back to the times they'd had when laughter had been in plentiful supply.

'Just okay? Think about it, Ella, isn't it a good thing that your father has been reassured that I'm the sort of guy who isn't going to disappear in the face of the responsibilities that have come his way?'

'You honestly didn't have to pass the test with so many flying colours.'

'I've never been a guy to do things by half-measures.'

'You've met my dad now. What happens when I meet your parents, Rocco? What are they going to make of this situation? Or will you keep them in the dark from it?'

'Keep them in the dark? That would be impossible.'

'How are they going to react to the fact that we won't be getting married, when they married because it made sense?'

Rocco's mouth thinned. How would his parents react? He already knew how, because he had already had that conversation. There had been no point delaying the inevitable, but it wasn't a conversation he had looked forward to, and it had gone as expected: a cold reception followed by an icy reminder of his uncle and what had happened when he had found himself trapped by a gold-digger.

'And that was *without* the complication of a child!' his mother had said in one of the few truly explosive reactions Rocco had ever heard.

Their cold fury had fired up a possessiveness inside him towards Ella which he had known was there without knowing just how powerful it was. Nothing about her could ever be described as greedy for money. Everything she said and did only confirmed that.

He felt her eyes on him and, for a split second, his heart opened up and warmed at feelings that lazily swirled inside him, defying logic. Logic said he wasn't built for the highs and lows of love. Logic said that his uncle had been the benchmark of how a loss of control could ruin lives. Logic told him that to marry and yet keep a distance was the way the marriage would work and, better than that, would thrive. He wouldn't pretend emotions that would never be there, and so she would never be disappointed because she couldn't access them. But she would be satisfied on every other front.

'I guess they would have expected you to get married to someone from the same social standing as you?'

'I'm sure that's exactly what they expected, but in life things don't always go according to plan.'

'They'll be bitterly disappointed that not only will you not be marrying the right type of girl but that that wrong type of girl is pregnant with your baby.'

'My parents' opinion belongs to them,' Rocco said, voice cooling as he thought about his parents. 'I hope I can change it but, if I can't, then I won't let it affect me or how I behave in this situation.'

'Really?'

'I don't have the same relationship you have with your father,' Rocco said quietly. 'I've looked at the interaction between the two of you. There's no hiding the deep love that's there, and I'm guessing your entire family unit was like this?'

'It was,' Ella agreed with a smile in her voice. 'Conor may have been as wild as anything sometimes, and Mum may have been dogged with health issues, but there was so much love there. When you say you don't have the same relationship…'

'I think I may have given some hints on that particular topic when we…were together.'

'Maybe.'

'The details may have been omitted but all the necessary bits were there.'

'I know you told me that you don't like Christmas. You can fill in the gaps now. It's not as though we aren't on a long journey together, for better or for worse.'

In the silence of the car, Ella found that she was intensely curious to hear more about him. The black and white picture was fading and in its place was the colour of a rounded, three-dimensional man.

'Fill in the gaps... I suppose you could say that Christmas in my family's palatial house wasn't all you might think it was cracked up to be.'

'No festive tree?'

'Several. All huge and all decorated by an outside company who always did an excellent job when it came to making them worthy of a magazine cover. There was never a time when we ever went out to physically buy a Christmas tree.'

'Even when you were a kid?'

'Never. Nor was there ever any excited opening of presents on Christmas morning. I always had one present given to me at breakfast on Christmas day, and I was allowed to open it once the dishes had been removed by staff. It was always expensive, and elaborate, and as soon as I opened my gift it was expected that I would go upstairs to play with it so that my parents could get on with the rest of the day.'

'What was the rest of their day?'

'There was always a lavish buffet luncheon open to

the usual great and good. Sometimes, they would bring their kids over and I would have company.'

'Am I allowed to feel sorry for you?'

Lulled into the ease of conversation which she remembered from when they were lovers, Ella settled into something that felt familiar and exciting at the same time.

'If that makes you happy. Does it?'

'I can't imagine what that must have been like.' Would he compare the experience he was going to have putting up a tree for her father to his experiences as a child? Would that serve to underline the differences between them? He said that he would never let his parents influence how he dealt with this sudden bombshell dropped into his well-ordered life, but could the kid who had grown up in a mansion be completely immune to his past experience?

He talked of marriage, but could he sidestep prejudices that must have been in place from birth really to accept someone like her? Or was she being judgemental, allowing her own personal fears to cloud the issue?

She wondered why those thoughts were playing in her mind at all when she'd decided not to marry him, when everything he said now confirmed *why* they could never be suited. But there was enough doubt about that decision forming in the back of her mind to keep the thoughts churning as the car pulled into the packed car park that serviced the garden centre.

'We're really worlds apart, aren't we?' she murmured as he opened the passenger door for her, automatically reaching to help her out of the car.

Squirming round to fetch her backpack by her feet, she

straightened to find that he had stilled and was looking at her with brooding intensity.

'Yes, we are.'

'What on earth did you ever see in me in the first place?' The thread of hurt forced its way back to the surface. 'Was I just a novelty toy you got to play with for a couple of weeks?'

The to-ing and fro-ing of people, kids, voices, laughter and, in the distance, the tinned sound of Christmas carols faded away. Ella could feel the burn of his dark eyes on her and it hit her that this man would be around for their child while she got on with her own life—except how easy would that be when she was emotionally involved with him?

'Never that, although…'

'No, don't say it.' She forced a laugh. 'I sense what you're going to say next isn't going to be one of those compliments that has me fainting with joy.'

'You made me laugh and you still do,' he murmured with a slow smile.

'I hope the festive spirit here doesn't give you too much of a headache. You'll find that when it comes to Christmas we do things in style in this part of the world.'

She made to clamber out but his hand kept her in place.

'Although, like I said before, you brought out something in me that I hadn't realised was there. For a while I was someone else, someone without the responsibilities that have always come with my upbringing, and I liked that *someone else*. I told you that I didn't have to come back here, Ella and that was the truth. I didn't. Maybe

I came back to be re-introduced to that *someone else* I found when we were together.'

'But I was never going to be a permanent part of your life, Rocco. You might have wanted to feel free again for a while, but you were always going to go away in the end.'

Their eyes tangled and she was the first to look away. He neither confirmed nor denied that statement. Of course he would never have hung around to have a proper relationship with her second time round. The guy wasn't into love and had been brought up on a diet of duty, with a suitable wife somewhere along the line, someone from the right background who knew how things worked in that rarified life of his.

But could she be wrong? Impatient even to think along those lines, Ella snapped out of her temporary trance and hopped out of the car.

'You honestly don't have to help me out of a car, Rocco. I'm not an invalid.' But she tempered that with a smile because the gesture was really quite appealing. 'Now, let's go find a tree. I'm warning you that, if you're not a fan of Christmas, you might find the overload of decorations a little alarming...and watch out for errant elves.'

She swept through revolving doors into the garden centre, which was awash with fairy lights. The smell of pine in the air was heady and aromatic and, of course, carols blared from loud speakers dotted here and there.

In the cold, dull winter light Rocco was a sight to behold, so tall, lean and sexy. People walking around him slanted curious glances in his direction because he stood out, his long black coat the last word in expensive elegance, and his tan a sharp contrast to the pale faces all around them.

'Don't you think it's incredible that we will have a child who will be able to enjoy the meeting of two very different cultures—Irish and Spanish?' he murmured, tucking her hand in the crook of his arm and covering it with his own.

'I hadn't thought of it like that.'

The remark was casual but there was an intimacy there that reminded her, again, of the tantalising thought of what it would feel like to be married to him. She'd been so sure of herself but now...this felt a lot less clear-cut.

She wondered whether that also had something to do with the way he had engaged with her taciturn father. It occurred to her that her dad would have hated Steve, with his easy smile, his ready charm and that habit he'd had of pushing his blond hair out of his eyes. Steve would also have been at a loss with her father because there wouldn't have been a single meeting point between the two and she doubted that her ex would have bothered to make much of an effort.

Which brought comparisons to mind as she glanced sideways at Rocco's commanding figure next to her. He was so much the superior person in every single respect. Truths concealed seemed less relevant. It made her wince to think how readily she had buried herself back here, recovering from the loss of her mother and from a heart broken by a guy she could barely remember because next to Rocco, he barely registered now on her radar.

'I don't think I've ever been anywhere like this before,' Rocco said, and she glanced up at his handsome face and smiled.

'More firsts for you?'

'They seem to come with the territory where you're concerned.' He smiled back down at her.

Her heart lurched in what felt like a perfect moment. To the left, a group of tiny schoolchildren, who were maybe five or six years old, were bunched in a choir belting out a Christmas carol with tuneless enthusiasm. Rocco paused, looked at them and slowly strolled in their direction, taking Ella with him, and she could feel the tightening of his body next to hers. Ella glanced up at his riveted expression. He was shorn of his sophisticated, self-assured charm and the cool, lazy, tough veneer that made people jump to attention.

Right now, as he stood silently watching the children sing, there was a naked curiosity on his face that made her pause and her heart constrict. He reached into his pocket, found some notes and put them into the brightly wrapped box in front of the choir, then he turned to her.

'Tree?'

'I'm surprised that cash is still accepted,' she said. 'I half-expected a card machine.'

'Is that a tradition here? The kids singing?'

'I told you we do things in style around here. I used to go to the same school as those kids. And, yes, it's a tradition, like the Christmas tree in the store and the festive meal for the people who have nowhere to go over Christmas. I know you've already chatted to Vera, and told her that your door is open to anyone who wants to talk to you about what's going to happen, and you've also decided to go overboard and make the store as festive as possible. Thank you for that.'

The kids were still heartily singing as she drew him towards the back of the garden centre where the trees stood upright in their containers, waiting for approval.

Here, it was relatively quiet. The cold pinched her face. The flakes of the past few days hadn't materialised into full-throttle snowfall but still hung in the air with the promise of it.

The feeling of Christmas was all around them: the sound of the children's voices; the busy laughter; the lights and feeling of good cheer. An impressive display of Santa, his sled and team of reindeer adorned the entrance to the centre.

'What do you think of that tree?' She pointed to one in the corner and went to inspect it.

'Seems small.'

'Maybe compared to twenty-foot statement pieces where you lived,' Ella said wryly. 'We never had a big one at home. It was all about the decorations. And the lights, of course.'

'Will it be the same without your brother here?'

'We'll do a video call on Christmas Day. I guess you'll be with your parents on Christmas day? You haven't said…'

'All in due course. Now, will they deliver this, or do I organise a driver to take it to the house?'

Ella burst out laughing. 'Don't be ridiculous. When you're in Rome, you have to do as the Romans do, and these Romans don't get drivers to deliver Christmas trees. It will be delivered to the house some time later this evening.'

'I think maybe a little sooner than that. I enjoy stricter timelines.'

He offered them a bumper donation to the Christmas choir fund and was duly rewarded with a tree that would arrive within the hour.

'Shall I tell you something? This is the first time I've ever felt any sort of Christmas spirit.'

Ella's breath hitched. He reached to stroke her face. She wanted him to kiss her so much it hurt, but he didn't, and it was all she could do not to pull him against her and kiss the living daylights out of him.

She didn't want his kindness and respect. She wanted passion. Should she give this a chance? Should she take what he was offering? He'd said that friends turned into lovers and not the other way round, but could they do a full circle? Could lovers become friends and then friends become lovers once again, but with the depth, commitment and love of two people destined for one another?

He said things that came straight from the heart and she knew, deep inside, that what he said was only for her and nothing to do with the fact that she was pregnant. She was sure of it! She didn't think that he even realised that. Maybe that was why she'd felt that powerful connection the very first time they'd really started talking to one another.

That was why his departure and the deceit she'd uncovered had been so devastating. It was also why she continued to be pulled towards him, yearning to go against what her head was telling her about lessons learnt.

The way he said that hadn't been just a statement of fact. Yes, he'd explained why Christmas meant so little to him, but there had been something achingly poignant when he'd told her that this was his first taste of real Christmas spirit.

'Sure you want to do the whole tree decorating thing with me and my dad?' she asked softly, resting her small hand on his arm.

'Why wouldn't I?'

'Because it's really not necessary,' she hedged awkwardly. 'Also...'

'Also?'

'Also if you're uncomfortable...' She laughed hesitantly.

'You're very sensitive, aren't you? Do you think I'm going to burst into tears in a moment of rare sentimentality?'

'I'd love to see that. But really, Rocco, you must have had a lonely childhood.'

Primed to react according to instinct, to put barriers into place, Rocco found that he couldn't because the usual safeguards weren't there. For a few seconds, he felt as though he was freefalling, then he regained control sufficiently to smile at her with wry self-deprecation.

'I coped, so don't feel too sorry for me. Now, shall we get some coffee? Breakfast? I noticed a café by the desk over there. Have you eaten?'

'I'm fine. There's no need to fuss.'

'I find it seems to come naturally with you being pregnant.'

'You sound surprised by that.'

'Who'd have thought?' Rocco half-murmured to himself. 'Okay, let's get back. Snow looks like it's beginning to get serious. We'll get the tree sorted and when that's done... I suppose we need to sit down and have a conversation about the details of our arrangement if marriage is not on the cards.'

As if she'd been doused by a bucket of cold water, Ella suddenly felt the sharp pang of fear at the prospect of not having this man in her life. Of seeing him disappear into the arms of some appropriate woman who would...what? Provide the sort of cold example of part-time surrogate motherhood that his own mother had, from the sounds of it? How did she feel about that? How did she feel about him no longer fussing around her or being in her life aside from slowly becoming a stranger whose only link would be the child they shared?

Did she want him moving on without her?

By the time they made it back, the tree was already at the house, and her father had positioned it in the usual place in the sitting room, by the front window. He bustled them out of the cold and hugged her and Ella hugged him back hard. Hugged him for the grief he had lovingly protected her from seeing when her mother had died, and for the hope and joy inside her because she knew that she was going to accept Rocco's marriage proposal.

Rocco watched this show of love with mixed feelings. Who was this man standing here, torn because all his ingrained and deeply embedded principles felt shadowy and ineffectual as he witnessed their open affection for one another? He'd found some other side of himself when he'd started his affair with Ella and it was still there, illogically defying a lifetime of indoctrination that had pointed him down the rigid path he had always been expected to follow. The path he had willingly *accepted* was the right one to follow.

He'd dropped all talk of marriage, but was discomforted when he thought about losing this link to someone he had grown to like, someone without the constraints that had ruled his life.

'Here, help with these.'

Rocco shrugged off uncomfortable thoughts and found a bundle of lights in his hands. 'What's this?'

'It's an absolute pig's ear of tangled Christmas tree lights! That's what happens when you don't pull them out for a year! Your job is to do your best to get them up and running. And don't tell me you've never done anything like that in your life before. You can see it as one of the festive season's little challenges!'

Rocco looked at the clear green eyes gazing at him with amusement and he smiled. The urge to touch her was overwhelming. The flare of panic he felt at her not accepting his marriage proposal was suddenly equally overwhelming.

'Now, a good challenge is something I've never been able to resist.'

Her eyes lingered on him just a little bit longer than necessary and the pink that infused her cheeks kickstarted a rush of physical desire, which was something he understood and could deal with. Easier than troublesome, introspective thoughts.

The air was sucked out of Ella as she gazed back at him, on some subconscious level tuning in to what he was feeling, which mirrored her own response—hot desire, a need to touch and be touched. Her breasts were suddenly heavier than normal, her nipples, darker and bigger in pregnancy, even more sensitive than they'd been.

Freed from the restraints of having to convince herself that Rocco was unsuitable for her, a liar who didn't deserve much of a second chance, was her body now reacting to the freedom that had come with her change of heart? Her breathing slowed.

'What about you?' he murmured into the electric silence. 'How are *you* with challenges?'

'G-good, thanks,' she stuttered.

'Shall I get on with the lights? You're distracting me.'

Ella blinked like an owl when he raised his hand and dangled the ball of Christmas lights in front of her, although his dark eyes never left her face for a second, not until they dipped to linger on her mouth.

The rest of the morning passed in a blur as they strung the lights and hung the decorations, and it was nearly one by the time her father decided to call it a day, because crops had no respect for Christmas traditions.

'But stay for dinner, young man,' he said over his shoulder before he left. 'Always plenty in this house when it comes to food.'

'I'll have to ask your daughter for permission.' Rocco turned to Ella.

'So...' he drawled, when her father had left. 'Think the tree was the right choice?'

'Amazing, and thanks for the lights.'

He moved to stand next to her so that they were both

gazing at the tree, and again he felt that peculiar hollowness inside him.

'The decorations...' he murmured.

'I know. Most of them are ancient, relics from childhood for me and Conor.'

He listened as she went through them, picking some of them out, smiling and reminiscing about times past and showing him a world he hadn't known existed because it was one he'd never encountered. The decorations were spread wide, dating back to childish paintings on cardboard with makeshift holes for hanging.

'So, do you say *yes*, Ella?'

Rocco looked down at her upturned face.

They had somehow drifted over to the deep, comfortable sofa by the fireplace. From here, Rocco could see unbroken greyness through the window and the stubborn flurries of light snow slanting in the thin afternoon light.

Ella didn't bother pretending to misunderstand his question.

'Yes. I'll marry you,' she told him quietly. Free to get physically close, she rested the palm of her hand on his chest, as if trying to gauge his heartbeat. 'I know...it comes with certain terms and conditions...' She waited a heartbeat for an interruption which didn't come. 'No love or romance or any of that other stuff...but you were right. This isn't just about the two of us now. This is bigger and it's something that calls for some sacrifice. And besides...'

'You're not making a mistake.'

Wasn't she? Ella couldn't have said but what she did know was that between a rock and a hard place a choice had to be made, and with this choice came the opportunity for her love to infect him, because they would be around one another, filling the spaces between them with laughter and affection. Those things were only a heartbeat away from love. If she held his hand for long enough, she could surely lead him there?

'I hope not.'

Rocco stayed the night.

He didn't know how he managed to make it through the remainder of the evening. He knew that the meal her dad prepared for them had tasted great. He knew that the snow had gathered momentum. He appreciated the Christmas tree, ablaze with light and the dozens of decorations that sat by the window, advertising a spirit of celebration and love that his family's grand tree never had. And, naturally, he knew that they had talked about marriage, and had been aware of her father's quiet approval.

He had ached to get to that bedroom, and when they made it there, after what had felt like hours of talking and eating, and eating and talking, he took his time.

No hurried sex with clothes being ripped off and strewn on the floor because desire overwhelmed finesse. He'd undressed her very slowly, removing each layer of clothing with solicitous, painstaking care.

Her body was ripe with their child. Her nipples were bigger and darker, her belly just beginning to show the soft roundness of pregnancy. He had buried himself in the soft down between her thighs, had sucked on her breasts and had caressed every part of her until, when neither of them could take any more, he had come in her.

He hadn't pushed back against her refusal to marry him. He'd waited. For a man who preferred the immediacy of action, the wait had proved fruitful.

Today, he thought much later, as he lay in bed with her head against his shoulder, had been a good one.

CHAPTER EIGHT

ELLA WOULD HAVE liked the honeymoon period to last for more than five and a half minutes but she had to admit to herself that that was never likely to happen.

They weren't leads in a romcom where eleventh-hour revelations occurred and love was shouted from the rooftops. He might be attracted to her—and her body burned when she remembered just how heatedly he had proven that—but this was a practical matter for him. After the night they'd spent together at her house, he'd almost immediately reminded her that things would have to be set in motion.

And, since then, Rocco had been true to his word. He had stayed for the night and the following morning he told her he would have to return to London.

'Come with me,' he urged quietly, his dark eyes intent and serious. 'Because we need to pin down timings and details of what happens next. Life for both of us is about to dramatically change, and I'm not a man to approach big changes in life without due diligence being done beforehand.'

He was standing fully dressed by the side of the bed at the crazily early hour of half-past six in the morning. It was still pitch-black outside. It could have been midnight. Ella was lying naked under the thick winter duvet, barely awake and still pleasurably indulging in drowsy thoughts of Rocco slowly beginning to love her the way she loved him. After the most wonderful and loving experience with him the night before, she was inclined to optimism.

She snapped out of that in a hurry.

'London?'

'I have a place there as well offices.'

Which brought home to her just how different his alter ego had been—the one with a small business concern in Madrid and an eye to elevating his position in life. The one who had rented a one-bed cottage to give her the illusion that that had been the most he could afford.

She knew it was stupid to dwell on those differences because the outward trappings didn't reflect the inner man who was one and the same. At least, they didn't most of the time. Right then, as he stood restlessly next to the bed, she could almost believe that man was morphing back into the autocratic businessman she had first encountered in that boardroom.

'Before we marry—and incidentally I feel that marriage should be as soon as possible—documents will have to be signed, preparations put in place. The usual paraphernalia of two people getting hitched.'

'Documents?'

She watched him hesitate, but only briefly. 'Financial stipulations. A pre-nup being top of the agenda.'

'A pre-nup? I wouldn't call that "the usual paraphernalia of two people getting hitched".'

'It is in my world. Would you be…amenable to signing one?'

'Of course.' But the atmosphere had changed subtly, even though she acknowledged that this was no different from what anyone with his kind of wealth would have suggested.

Especially bearing in mind that she didn't come from the same place as him; didn't share the same social standing. The rules of the game were completely different.

He hadn't dwelled on those differences. When he was with her, he was relaxed, as at home in her dad's house and with her dad as anyone could be, but those differences existed. She just had to think back to when he had described the sort of woman his parents would expect him to marry.

Love, though, overcame everything.

'Rocco, I wouldn't dream of trying to get money out of you if…if for some reason… *No.* I'm just not that kind of person.'

'I'm not doubting you but…'

'But rules are rules?' She shrugged, choosing to give him the benefit of the doubt. 'I get it. Just about. It's a weird world you live in, but I suppose you always have to be on high alert for gold-diggers. Also, yes, I'll come to London. When? And where do you want to meet?'

'I thought you could come to my place.' He moved towards her, leant over and kissed her gently on the forehead before pushing her hair back. 'I'm looking forward to marrying you,' he murmured. 'I'm really glad you changed your mind. You're doing the right thing— I know that—and so am I. The right thing for our baby.

I realise you feel you're making a sacrifice, perhaps in ways that I'm not, and don't imagine that I don't appreciate that. I do.'

Beautiful words. Her heart softened.

'Okay. I'll sort a train out.'

At which Rocco had looked at her with amusement. 'Consider public transport a thing of the past,' he said with surprise in his voice. 'Too uncomfortable in your condition.'

'Really?' Ella smiled. 'Maybe you should try telling that to the thousands of them heading here, there and everywhere on buses and trains and tubes.'

'I could arrange for my helicopter to get you. A driver can collect you from here and—'

'No!' Her voice was terser than intended because she had a sudden vision of letting go of the sort of life she'd always had, floundering in a new world order in which she didn't belong. 'I'd die of fright in a helicopter.'

'I also have a private jet at my disposal.'

'Rocco, a commercial flight will suit me just fine.'

It had felt like a small win for her world over his. But, she fleetingly thought, how long would that last?

It had taken a little longer than the original twenty-four hours planned for Ella to head to London. Important meetings had demanded Rocco's absence from the country, so it was five days after they had agreed the visit, at a little after six in the evening, that Ella stood in front of an impressive Regency house, one of about twenty that formed an imposing crescent that curved in a semi-circle around a private, gated park manicured to within an inch of its life.

The houses were fronted with perfectly symmetrical cream columns. Even the lamp posts outside every three houses appeared to stand to attention, respectful of their grand surroundings. There wasn't a Christmas tree in sight, and certainly no inflatable Santas on sleds gaily announcing from the tops of the buildings that it was the festive season. There *were* wreaths on the doors, however, with lush foliage and just the right shades of metallic accents to contrast nicely against the highly polished black front doors.

It was hard to marry the man who had joked around with her dad and been intrigued at the kids singing carols with the man who lived behind that imposing door. It was deathly quiet. The cars parked outside were eye-wateringly high-end—cars that belonged to people who also had private jets and helicopters at their disposal.

Ella pressed the doorbell and, before she could remove her finger from the buzzer, the door opened and there he was, standing in front of her, and her heart leapt.

It was freezing outside but he was in a pair of loose, black jogging bottoms and a tee-shirt. Apparently it was summer in Belgravia, even if it was the middle of December everywhere else.

'Ella...'

Rocco smiled and stood aside so that she could brush past him, pulling a small case on wheels behind her. She smelled of a fragrant scent which, he suspected, was nothing more than the smell of her shampoo. He was ridiculously pleased to see her because, even though it had only been a matter of days since he'd returned to London, only to jet off immediately to New York, she'd been on his mind. He'd missed her and he put that down to the fact that they were on a completely different footing now. Naturally she would be on his mind because their relationship had undergone a seismic change. Plus, their love-making had been...sensational.

'I still think you should have let my driver bring you to London,' he said without preamble as she moved gracefully into his house and looked around her with an expression he couldn't quite read.

'This is an amazing place.' She turned full-circle and then crooked her head at one of his paintings. 'Is that a real Hockney on the wall?'

'All the artwork in here is the real deal.'

Rocco went to relieve her of her coat and noticed she was wearing a million layers underneath. He itched to get them all off. However, he'd had time to think, and he was going to play it cool. Attraction or no attraction, this was first and foremost an arrangement that made sense and not a searing tale of high romance. He didn't want her getting the wrong impression. He didn't want her expectations to be built to levels he wouldn't be able to meet.

He didn't want her falling in love with him.

Of course, she wouldn't do that, not when she was coming from a place of mistrust because of the circumstances under which they had met. Not when he'd had to convince her to marry him. Not when she had been through disillusionment with a partner and was wary of emotional involvement with the wrong guy.

But still... Right now she was independent, and wanted nothing from him beyond what he had put on the table, but that was *right now*. He didn't want her investing in him emotionally as time moved on. He didn't want her to become the sort of clingy, demanding wife who expected shows of devotion and was disappointed if they failed to materialise. He didn't have it in him to be that sort of man, even if he could fill in the blanks in all the other areas that mattered, and he knew it would be a fine line between disappointment and eventually filing for divorce.

So he would play it cool. Even though, right now, as he looked at her turn full circle in his vast hallway, he was anything but cool. In fact, he had never felt hotter.

'You should shed the layers, Ella. I keep this place well heated in winter.'

'So I notice. I never asked, but you must have been freezing when you stayed the night. There's always been a strict policy at home of layering up in winter because only namby-pambies rely on central heating twenty-four seven to keep warm.'

'I incline to the policy that there's no point freezing to death to prove a point. By the way, I hope you don't think I'm a *namby-pamby...*'

Ella reddened. 'You *should* be,' she said truthfully and reddened a little more when he strolled towards her with a wolfish, curling smile.

'I'm one of a kind,' he murmured, sliding his fingers into her hair and cupping her face. 'Haven't you realised that by now?'

Desire surged and memories of how she had felt against him, pregnant and naked, filled him up until he was drowning in the need to bury himself in her. He breathed in deeply and pulled back to a place of self-control.

'Want me to give you the guided tour? Or can that wait? You must be tired after your journey.'

'I guess the guided tour can wait and I'm not tired. The train was very comfortable. It's a novelty to travel first class.'

'You make me want to show you all the things that money can buy,' he confessed in a roughened undertone and she burst out laughing.

'You're so shallow, Rocco Mancini. How did you ever cope with being Jose Rivero?'

'Women are impressed with what money can buy.'

'Well, to parrot what you've just said, *I'm one of a kind.*'

She was, and he was pleased and satisfied that maybe the gap between the man he was and the man he'd pretended to be was closing. She was smiling at him, and for a few seconds he was deprived of speech. 'I've ordered in food—French. I hope that's fine with you?'

'Lovely.'

'And you've been eating, haven't you?'

'I've been eating. I know you're fully engaged with the pregnancy but you don't have to caretake me. You've phoned a thousand times since you left Ireland.'

Rocco flushed. 'What's surprising about that? You're having my baby. I'm concerned for your well-being. Naturally, I'm going to phone to find out how you are.'

'Yes, it's very sweet.'

'I'm not a sweet person. Anyone would tell you that.' Sweet? Never a description that had been applied to him. 'Have you missed me?' he asked in a husky, lazy voice which matched the look he shot her from under his lashes. 'Because I've missed you.'

'It hasn't been very long... How was New York?'

'My libido doesn't keep tabs on time, and New York was New York.'

He stroked the side of her face and smiled when her eyelids fluttered and her lips parted. Their kiss was soft and sweetly captivating. Sliding gently between his lips, her tongue was a lingering caress that did amazing things to his body.

He tugged her closer so that he could feel her against him and he knew that she could feel his stiff erection pushing through the jogging pants he was wearing. 'Want to take this further?' he growled. He guided her hand to his erection and encouraged her to massage it.

'Rocco...' she breathed.

'I like it when you say my name. Your accent...turns me on.'

'Just my accent?'

'Everything about you turns me on. Why do you think this is going to work so well? This thing between us... this chemistry...makes what we have more than just an arrangement because you're pregnant.'

But, Ella suddenly thought, that was it, wasn't it? It was just an arrangement in which the added bonus was sex. She now had so much more of a complete picture of the man he was, the man with the background that had shaped his beliefs, who was quietly convinced that to love and to be vulnerable in love was something he could never do. This would be a marriage on his terms and, if she hoped that she could reach inside and slowly guide him to a place where he would give without thought the love he now felt he couldn't give, then she would have to be wary of losing herself in the process.

She might have put Steve into perspective, downplayed the heartbreak she had felt because he had been so insignificant compared to Rocco, but the disappointment in that relationship, in the why and the how it had failed, was very real. He had let her down, and she had to protect herself against being let down by Rocco.

Yes, there was a sincerity about him that Steve had never possessed underneath the glib charm, but there was a lot of road to be travelled before she could fully trust him.

He had concealed the truth from her once, whatever genuine excuses he had made about that.

But how she was tempted to toss in the towel and go for broke on the trust front...

'We have time for...you know...all of that. And, actually, I'm quite hungry.'

'Yes. Dinner.'

'You shouldn't have gone to all this trouble,' was the first thing she said when she was confronted with the elaborate French meal that had been prepared by one of Rocco's favourite chefs of a Michelin-starred restaurant a stone's throw away.

'What trouble? Everything was delivered in heat-proof containers, ready for the oven. I didn't have to do anything.' He shrugged. 'Jean Claude is a personal friend and, whenever I want something, he's always happy to help out.'

'*The* Jean Claude?'

'The very same.' Rocco nodded at his granite-topped table and watched as she warily sat down, looking around her all the while.

He suddenly realised that he was so accustomed to the very pinnacle of luxury that he rarely noticed his surroundings. Now, though, he looked at his own house through her eyes: a sprawling London townhouse in one of the most expensive postcodes in the capital. Close to eight-thousand square feet of prime real estate. He had originally bought it because it was conveniently located for his offices, and because it was light and airy, and that reminded him of Spain.

Every room had soaring ceilings. The artwork was priceless, the sort of artwork many people might keep locked away for insurance purposes, but for him, what was the point of that? The furnishings were pale and minimalist, every single piece bespoke, and had been chosen and sourced globally by the most expensive interior design team in the city.

When he remembered her father's cosy place—the Christmas tree with the hand-made decorations; the old, comfortable sofas; the weathered kitchen table and the feel of *love* imbued into everything—Rocco felt something pierce him deep inside. Ella would be entering his highly refined, wealthy orbit. It was a world to which he was wedded and she would be as well. The comparison to the one she inhabited now, the one she had grown up around, and his own could not have been more stark.

Another reason to make sure that they didn't start this very important next step with her harbouring any romantic illusions that he would ever become the sort of cosy, homey guy she had probably been brought up to seek out as a mate. He couldn't change his destiny, and experience had taught him that it was best served with rigorous discipline and control. He was who he was and she would, essentially, have to fall in line.

He served the food, waving down her offers of help. Then, when they were facing one another at the table, he said, gently but in a businesslike voice, 'To recap what we briefly touched on before, Ella—documents have to be signed. I can make an appointment for us to see lawyers first thing tomorrow so we can get the ball rolling on the financial front.'

'I've only just got here!' She dived into the food and glanced up at him from under her lashes. 'What's happened to the guided tour?'

'The paperwork comes first, I'm afraid.'

'You could always just bring whatever it is I have to sign here and I'll sign it.' She shrugged. 'We don't need to get lawyers involved, do we? Didn't we say it would all be a little less formal?'

'We very much do. And besides, in my world, lawyers are *always* involved.' He looked at her as she continued eating and wondered whether he could detect a certain stiffening of her shoulders. 'It's not just about the pre-nup. It's what happens with the child in the event of a break-up of any kind, from separation to divorce. Financial arrangements need to be put in place along with something that is legally binding on custody.'

'Rocco, I just can't think that far ahead! Our baby isn't even born yet!' But she couldn't help but see the pattern of someone who left nothing to chance—except, as it turned out, contraception. Whether he liked it or not, control was something that could end up very slippery.

'They're just precautionary measures.' Rocco flushed. 'There's no avoiding them.'

'I'm happy to sign whatever you want me to sign if it's to do with money, because I don't care about the money. But I'm not signing away rights to my own child in the event that something happens somewhere along the line and we don't end up together. I'm just not prepared to do that.'

Rocco paused. He lowered his eyes. 'Like I said, it's just a precaution. My background dictates certain measures be taken.'

'Or else what? Is the world going to stop turning if you don't take those measures?'

'Hardly, but—'

'I won't do it, Rocco.'

Rocco sighed, flung both hands in the air and shot her a frustrated glance from under his lashes. 'Why are you so stubborn?'

'I just can't plan every single detail, and besides, I have to stand up for myself, Rocco. Look around you—all this privilege and wealth. I can't afford to let you dominate the narrative. I can't afford to be overwhelmed by all of this.'

'But we have to find a way past arguing about things that have already been accepted. We're going to be married.'

'That doesn't mean that I don't have to protect myself,' Ella said evasively.

She was skating on thin ice. Yes, they were going to be married, and she wanted the marriage to work, and not just because it made sense. Lots of things in life *made sense* but that didn't mean that one was compelled to take those roads.

She wanted to hope a piece of his heart was willing to open up, and she knew that all it would take would be a chink, but to show how she felt now… How would he react? He thought he knew all the answers and, what he didn't know, he could somehow predict and so control.

How would he react if he knew how she felt about him? Would the marriage proposal come off the table? Now that she had accepted it, she couldn't face the thought of not being married to him. She'd come full circle. From bitterness and scepticism, he had managed to prove himself to her and, his having done that, she had let hope creep in. But hope and complete idiocy were two different things and she still had to have some safeguards in place.

'What are you protecting yourself from?'

'From landing up in a place where I don't know the rules of the game and there's no one to show them to me.'

'Where do you think I'm going to be during all of this? Haven't I proved to you that you can count on me?'

'You don't understand. It was easy for you to slide into my life, to charm my dad. But what I'm facing is completely different. I mean, have you even told your parents about…about everything?'

'I'm going to break the glad tidings to them later tonight,' Rocco said, rising to his feet and doing a half-hearted job of tidying the table.

He could feel the sudden tension in his shoulders because this was a blatant lie. Or at least, a very creative way of dealing with the truth. But he decided, without analysing it too deeply, it would be better to give her the final reassurance she needed that she hadn't been manoeuvred into a marriage she hadn't originally wanted.

And he hadn't *manoeuvred her*, he told himself, without a shred of inner doubt. He'd just allowed her to see that he could be counted on. He'd allowed her to be persuaded by all the advantages she and their baby would have if she tied the knot with him.

If he'd presented the situation to his parents earlier as a fait accompli, then likewise he'd been smoothing the path for them. All told, it was the best way of handling everything, and he was accustomed to handling things in the most efficient way possible.

'There's dessert.' He changed the subject as he fetched some bowls from the cupboard. When he turned round, he released a short sigh of relief, because her face had softened.

'Sometimes I see life in black and white,' he admitted. 'A lot of people imagine that to be born into a life of privilege must be pretty amazing—holidays to far-flung places, the best of everything life has to offer—but in my case it was a rigid life without much scope for...moving too far outside the box. The very gilded box.'

'And that's why you felt so free when you didn't have to be the person other people expected things from... when we met.'

'We worked for one another, Ella. We just didn't see this coming. All I'm doing is dealing with it in the only way I know how.'

'Which doesn't mean that I don't have concerns. I mean...is there a timeline for going to see your parents?

If they don't know anything just yet, do they expect that you'll be spending Christmas with them?'

'I'll arrange for us to see them before Christmas. I'm guessing you'll want to spend Christmas with your dad and, if I'm honest, so would I.' He shot her a crooked smile. 'Now I've had a little bit of what Christmas should feel like, I'm hungry for more.'

Ella smiled and relaxed. 'Just think of how much fun it'll be when there's three of us.' She accepted the chocolate gâteau and fork that he handed her on a small plate.

Doubts eased away. 'I could get used to all this fussing even though, naturally, it's not necessary, and on principle I object.'

'I admire a woman of principle.'

Ella could feel her whole body react to his proximity as he dragged a chair over and waited until she'd finished the cake before dabbing some stray chocolate from the side of her mouth. She sucked in her breath and had to resist the temptation to wrap her arms around him and bury her head against him.

'Okay, guided tour...' he growled against her neck and she started with dismay.

'What *now*?'

'To my bedroom. First and only stop will be my bed.' He scooped her off the chair and ignored her half-hearted protest. He walked and kissed her at the same time, fired up by her tiny, little whimpers of pleasure.

Ella lost herself in her body's urgent, driving needs. She was on fire by the time they made it to the bedroom. He laid her on the mattress, stepped back to look at her and she basked under his hungry gaze and was ready as he pushed up the top. She wasn't wearing a bra. She quivered as she clamped his mouth onto her nipple and sucked, his tongue rasping on the stiffened bud, driving her crazy with pleasure. She was barely aware of him undressing her, not completely, but enough. Enough to trace her no longer flat stomach with his hand, to ease off the loose trousers she was wearing, followed by her panties. She was so wet for him. She flung back her head, closed her eyes and groaned with the anticipation of being pleasured, opening her legs to accommodate the mouth she knew would find the throbbing bud of her clitoris. Her body ached and yearned for him.

His tongue found the perfect spot and she moaned as he flicked it against her clitoris, over and over until she could feel the steady build of an orgasm. She couldn't hold back. She wanted him deep in her, but she couldn't resist his demanding tongue, and she moaned and shuddered against his mouth as she came.

Shaken, satisfied and drowsy as desire slowly ebbed away Ella blinked like an owl and then sighed. 'Rocco...'

She shot him a hooded glance as he straightened, still staring at her with a little smile, and in that smile she could read all sorts of very acceptable levels of appreciation. Ella shuffled herself back into something resembling a state of dress and yawned as exhaustion began creeping in.

'You're tired.'

'I... I'm okay.'

'You need a nice hot bath.'

'You're fussing again.'

'You like it,' he teased and she thought, a little uncomfortably, *yes, far too much...*

He scooped her up and took her directly to an *en suite* bathroom that was as big as a football field and very, very modern. There was no glass door concealing a shower cubicle but a huge wet room, a massive bath...and even a comfortable chair against the wall big enough for two.

He sat her on the chair while he ran the bath and tested the water. She thought, *if, in a fortnight, you could find part of yourself you'd never accessed before, then over time, with a child uniting us, is it really so much to think that I could bring out the person I know you are?*

She could have lost herself in that daydream for ever. Turning it into reality felt like a tiny heartbeat away.

'You relax here for a bit,' he said, pushing her hair back and helping her into the warm, deep, foamy water. 'I'll bring your bag up and then I have a couple of work calls to make. Climb into bed. I won't be long.'

He was gone before she could reply and she did as told. She enjoyed a long, lazy bath. Like the rest of the house, the enormous bathroom was in pale marble, only broken by a granite square defining the wet room. The towels were big, fluffy white ones and beautifully warm from the heated towel rail. She felt like a special guest in a very expensive five-star hotel.

When she'd had her bath, she clambered into bed and was nodding off when Rocco eventually returned.

'Sorry I took a little longer than I expected. One of the calls I made was to my parents.'

'Ah. How did it go? How did they take the news? They

must have been shocked. Did they ask a lot of questions about us?'

'Some, as to be expected. I've arranged for us to go and pay them a visit. It will be a fleeting one.'

'You've actually arranged a date? Already?'

'There's no point delaying the inevitable,' Rocco said wryly.

'Why not? We could delay it for a bit longer. Let them get used to the idea of their one and only son getting married to the unsuitable girl he got pregnant.'

'Getting used to that might take them a while.'

'That's not very reassuring for me.'

'You have nothing to worry about. We'll be there two days and, while we're there, you can count on me to shield you from any awkward interaction.'

'Awkward interaction?' Ella laughed nervously.

'Nothing that can't be dealt with,' Rocco soothed. 'But you have to understand that they're very traditional and they've had set ideas about the direction of my life. Including the sort of woman who might eventually wear my ring.'

'And you've never led them to think that you might ever want to follow a different route…'

'Like I said, my life was set in stone from a very young age.'

'So when is this visit going to take place?'

'Tomorrow late-afternoon. My private jet is on standby.'

Private jet? Standby? Just for a second Ella had a fleeting and vaguely uneasy vision of the life she had signed up to. It wasn't going to be anything like the one she was accustomed to living. She'd known that, of course, but she'd been lulled into a sense of security because he'd been on her turf and in her territory. Now, she would be entering a different world, and she had to fight the chasms between them opening up around the seeds of hope that had taken root.

He would be by her side. He'd assured her that everything would be okay. And she believed him because he had proved that he was the man she'd thought he was.

CHAPTER NINE

ELLA HAD HER first taste of how the uber-rich lived first thing the following morning.

She was swept into a world of personal shopping, where the normal trudge from store to crowded store was exchanged for the emptiness of the high-end boutique and the fawning subservience of assistants bending over backwards to show her the latest pieces. There were no price tags on any of the clothing.

'I have enough clothes to last two days,' Ella had pointed out.

'My parents are aficionados of formal attire,' Rocco had told her. 'I've never seen either of them in a pair of jeans.'

Ella had immediately got the message: cargo pants, dungarees, baggy jumpers and her capacious winter coat weren't going to do. She ended up with several outfits, shoes for the evening and a bag, only escaping a trip to a beauty salon because they'd been running out of time. She wasn't sure whether she'd enjoyed the experience or whether she'd felt manipulated into a spending spree she wasn't altogether comfortable with—even though she belatedly realised that this sort of spree, so ridiculously uncustomary for her, would probably become the norm.

Now, as they sat waiting for Rocco's private jet to take off, Ella glanced down at the beautiful pale-grey cashmere trouser outfit she wore and the black designer coat casually slung over the cream leather seat on the other side of the aisle. She felt a little faint when she took in the rich wood veneer of the private jet, the plush seating arranged in little clusters for maximum comfort and the large windows with electronic shades, everything the last word in luxury.

Next to her, Rocco was scrolling through his phone, catching up on emails.

'I feel like an imposter,' she said, turning to him.

Rocco stopped what he was doing and swivelled to look at her.

'Why?' Of course, he knew why. It had been impossible not to notice her bemusement underneath the quiet compliance as she'd been shown outfit after outfit in the sort of exclusive shops in which he doubted she'd ever set foot before in her life. And now she was sitting next to him on his private jet.

She'd wanted to look at the windows of the big department stores, which were dressed lavishly for Christmas, but they hadn't had time and he'd felt like Scrooge as he'd firmly guided her back to his waiting chauffeur.

He'd thought of the department store where she worked and how proud she'd been of the Christmas tree and the effort the staff had poured into decorating it, knowing it would be the last one to grace the foyer. He'd recalled her own Christmas tree and the warmth and love between her father and her as they had pulled out the decorations and taken a trip down memory lane with each and every one. He'd watched her gaze up at the lights in Knightsbridge as they'd been driven through the congested streets, where throngs of shoppers flanked the slow-moving traffic.

'I don't belong in this world,' she said bluntly.

'It's the same world as yours,' Rocco returned. 'You're only wearing slightly different clothing.'

'The closest I've ever got to a private jet is when I've seen one in a movie.'

'Aren't you enjoying the experience?' He said this as it taxied and then roared upwards. He raised his voice and continued to look at her, easing her gently towards an understanding of the life she was going to occupy.

'I guess there are no crowds at a packed terminal. Have you ever endured a winding queue at a terminal anywhere?'

'No.'

'What's it like to live your life, Rocco?'

'Very, very good now that you're in it and pregnant with my baby.' He reached out to cover her hand with his and smiled, a soothing, reassuring smile.

Ella closed her eyes and relaxed in her seat, with his hand still covering hers. She'd been so hesitant about accepting this marriage proposal but he'd waited patiently for her to make her mind up, and had taken his time to show her all the sides of his personality so that she could see what a dependable husband he would make—and a dependable husband would become the devoted dad.

And with both of those...well...who knew where things might eventually end when the beginnings were auspicious? What had started in deception, the thing that had so devastated her, had ended in this happy place. She would meet his parents and, if they were a little reserved to start with, she was sure they would eventually warm to her. Or at least accept her. Surely? Besides, he would be by her side and they wouldn't be staying for long. How objectionable could they be when they'd only have a very small dose of her to deal with?

'I hope your parents like me, even if it's eventually.' She voiced her thoughts aloud as the jet sped towards their destination.

Rocco squeezed her hand. Personally, his thoughts were more in the direction of 'all in the fullness of time' but his parents were far too well-bred to openly voice any disapproval.

'They will.' His voice was reassuringly persuasive.

'What if they don't?'

'I've never seen the point in dealing with hypothetical situations. Always best to wait until something happens and then deal with it, rather than creating a range of possible scenarios and getting worked up.'

'That's rich coming from the guy who was happy to project to a future where we had other partners,' Ella said absently, chewing her lip and frowning.

She briefly conjured up one of those hypothetical scenarios he had talked about. What if she'd dug her heels in and refused to marry Rocco, the son and heir to the family fortune that needed protecting? Would she have made this trip out to Spain now? Or would they have tried to convince their son to walk away from a child he had accidentally fathered, one who would have remained illegitimate? They were clearly traditionalists to the bone. Was she only going out to see them because she had agreed to marry their son at long last?

There was fertile ground here for all sorts of wild imaginings, but she shut the door to it, because she was now on a road and there was no turning back.

'We still have to discuss all the details of our marriage.' She turned to him and met his dark gaze steadily. 'Whatever you say, your world couldn't be more different than mine. It's not just a simple case of things being different superficially but the same deep down. You've seen where I come from, seen the life I've been accustomed to.'

'I admit some changes might be on the horizon.'

'I can't live a life of spending money and being pampered,' she told him bluntly. 'You asked me whether I'd enjoyed the day. As a one off, it was an experience, but I wouldn't want that to be my entire life.'

'What are you proposing?'

'I want to carry on working.'

'Ella, maybe we could postpone this discussion for later, when I'm not having to shout over the roar of a plane engine?'

'I feel like I'm on a roller coaster,' Ella returned with a frown. 'Yes, I'm really happy that you're taking an interest in this pregnancy...that was never something you expected or asked for...'

'This feels like well-trodden ground.'

'Now we're on our way to see your parents and that feels like I'm just a little bit higher on the roller coaster. If I'm not careful I'll be at the top, I'll have lost sight of the ground beneath me and, by the time I come hurtling back down, planet Earth won't bear any resemblance to the place I left behind. And Rocco...? That scares me.'

'That's very descriptive, Ella,' Rocco said thoughtfully. 'But, okay. I understand where you're coming from. Do you think holding down a job is worth the effort? Whatever you earn will be a pittance in the grand scheme of things. Also, I would want you to devote time to our child. I...'

'Yes?' There was sudden insistence in her voice.

'I know how sidelining a child to the safekeeping of strangers can have an effect,' Rocco said roughly. 'I wouldn't want to see...that outcome for any child of mine.'

There was an electric silence during which Ella looked at him, taking in the dark stain on his cheekbones, the sudden tightening of his well-shaped mouth and an air of vulnerability that was so rarely apparent in him.

Her heart constricted as once again she was exposed to a past that had doubtless been lonely for a small child, however much money had been thrown at him. It was another glimpse that made her feel so connected to him. She impulsively reached out to link her fingers through his, half-expecting him to make some deflecting, jokey remark about not wanting her to feel sorry for him, but he just squeezed her hand in response and gazed at her with a shuttered expression.

'Can I tell you something, Rocco?'

'Depends.'

'On what?'

'On whether you think I'll like what you want to tell me.'

He grinned but his dark eyes were wary and she smiled back. 'I'm being serious,' she said.

'That sounds ominous but go ahead.'

'First of all, when I say I want to work, the money would have nothing to do with it. It would be about mental stimulation. I would be very happy to get involved with some kind of volunteer work. And it would never be a full-time occupation. I would always put our child first and foremost. I know that there would be a nanny of sorts and, as long as I get to say who that nanny is and what their duties are, then that's fine.'

'That sounds reasonable enough,' Rocco murmured.

'Something else. Can I ask what sort of woman you envisaged yourself marrying? Or rather, let me rephrase that, was there already someone lined up for you in true "marriage of convenience" style?'

The silence stretched and Ella's mouth tightened because that silence spoke volumes. 'Forget I asked that.'

'What do you want me to say? I never imagined I would end up with an Ella but, while we're going down this road, not that there's a point to it, did *you* think you would end up with a guy like me? Someone who made you feel as though you were on a roller-coaster ride?'

'I guess not.' But Ella thought that roller-coaster rides, however terrifying, could also be exhilarating. And addictive. And all sorts of things when one got used to it and started concluding that life without the roller-coaster ride was unthinkable.

She wished she hadn't asked the question of him because she wouldn't want to hear it confirmed in stark terms that someone like her would never have been on his wish list. She didn't like to be reminded why, exactly, she was sitting on a private jet next to him because, cravenly, she wanted to hold onto the belief that they were destined to be together.

She'd invested in her dreams and her hopes and she stubbornly refused to let go. Was she being a blind fool? Was her optimism misplaced? But no. He hadn't tried to force her hand. He'd respected her decision to turn down his marriage proposal and had allowed her the space to make up her mind. He'd been the decent guy who had more than compensated for the cardboard cut-out creep she'd thought he was when she'd discovered the truth about him.

'I guess we can fine-tune the details,' she said, voice raised over the sound of the jet engine, 'In the next few days. Meanwhile, tell me about your house. What can I expect?' She hid her frown under a smile and banished unwelcome thoughts.

Nothing could have prepared Ella for what confronted her when Rocco's chauffeur finally pulled through a pair of imposing wrought-iron gates that led into sprawling gardens with manicured lawns, fountains and statues. The sort of place where a person could be forgiven for getting out their purse because they might have to pay to get inside and look around.

When she lost count of the windows, she decided it was no longer a house, it was a palace—which she should have expected, given everything he'd said, but which she discovered she really hadn't at all.

Tall arches and a series of marble columns were emblazoned with intricate stone carvings, and everything drew the eye to the magnificent double-door entrance. The grand windows were fronted with iron balconies, all as intricate as the stone carvings, lacy in their details. There were rows and rows of them, perfectly proportioned and as precise as an architectural drawing.

She stopped and stared. Her heart was beating fast and her mouth was dry. She was glad for the steadying grasp of Rocco's hand as he linked his fingers through hers.

'Don't worry,' he said with more hope than expectation. 'It's going to be fine.'

'Have you described me to your parents?'

'Why would I have done that?'

'They might be in for a shock.'

'They'll handle it.' Rocco shrugged. 'They've dealt with shocks before.' But he could feel the nervous shakiness of her hand in his. What could he say? It was a necessary hurdle and they wouldn't be there for very long.

'How can you be so cool and collected at a time like this?'

Rocco didn't say anything. Instead, he pressed the doorbell and heard it reverberate. One of the many servants, who did everything from clean to cook to tend the vast acreage of maintained lawns, would answer the door. Sure enough, his favourite, Jorge, did so and bowed deferentially.

His parents were in the casual sitting room having drinks, he was told, and would expect them both to join them at seven sharp. Only then, message delivered, did Jorge smile broadly at Rocco, ushering him in, and then greeting Ella with even more deference when she was introduced.

When Rocco glanced at Ella, he could see that she was shocked at the lack of ebullient welcome.

'My parents,' he murmured, leaning into her, 'Are slightly different to your father.'

'Are they excited to have you here for a couple of days at Christmas?'

'Come on,' was his non-committal response. 'I'll be in my usual suite of rooms. We can freshen up and then join them for pre-dinner drinks.'

If the boutiques with the fawning saleswomen, the chauffeur-driven cars and the private jet told a tale of wealth, then this *palace* and non-appearing parents told an even starker story of the differences between Rocco and her.

She gazed around her as he ushered her away from the front door. The hall was vast, with high ceilings and a massive chandelier that cast a mellow glow over highly polished marble floors. It should have been breathtaking but it felt like a mausoleum.

Ahead was a sweeping double staircase and, to the side, an over-sized Christmas tree, professionally decorated and there to impress. It was as coldly beautiful as the rest of what she saw. The perfect tree, branches dense and full, stretched up, up, up towards the ornate ceiling and decorated in a thousand delicate, hand-blown glass baubles in shades of red, gold and ivory. The thousands of golden lights twined around the tree reflected off the polished floors and crystal chandeliers above.

'I can't believe you grew up here,' she whispered.

'In between boarding school and trips abroad.'

'I'm beginning to understand what you meant when you said your parents liked formal attire. Jeans would look out of place here.'

Ella wanted him to talk, wanted to hear his voice, because it might have distracted her from the nerves gripping her now like a vice. She half-listened as he described the dining room, the ballroom used for highly formal occasions, the original stained glass on the first floor and the gold-leafed ceilings that dated back over a hundred years. There was a library stocked with first-edition classics and a private study that overlooked the manicured lawns at the back. As a boy, he had used it to work in it, he told her.

'There were peacocks back then,' he said with a certain amount of wistfulness. 'Sadly, no more. Still, the black swans on the private lake remain.'

As they walked up the impressive staircase, her eyes strayed to classic Spanish paintings and tapestries. They emerged onto the broad corridor of the first floor, and she gasped at the stretch of wall comprised entirely of a hand-painted mural depicting some era in Spanish history: horses, men in armour and stylised trees and castles.

She suspected a legion of servants tended to the mansion and its grounds, yet a ghostly silence hung over the exquisite palace. Aside from the terrifyingly huge Christmas tree in the hall, anyone would think that the festive season had bypassed the palace completely.

Rocco's suite was as big as her dad's entire house.

'I'll leave you to get ready,' he said. He glanced at his watch, then back at her. She looked lost. 'One of the housekeepers will knock in an hour and take you down to join my parents. I'll be there. Is that all right with you? I expect I should have a little down time with them before you join us.'

Ella smiled and walked towards him. He was so tall, so commanding, and had seemed so curiously distant towards his parents, but wanting to see them without her made sense, at least for a bit. She could more easily relate to this person.

'Of course you want to see your parents without me! You don't have to feel awkward about that.'

'I wouldn't say I felt awkward.'

'An hour will be more than enough. As long as I don't have to find my way through this place.' She smiled a watery smile. 'Then I'll be fine to join you later. If I have to locate whatever drawing room you're in, then there isn't a satnav on earth that's going to work. I'll be wandering the corridors for the rest of my life.'

'That would be the last thing I'd want.'

Ella's breath hitched in her throat as his dark eyes roamed over her with warm appreciation, reminding her of just how much she loved this guy. She thought of a lifetime of nights together and that gave her just the right amount of backbone she needed.

'Okay,' she said a little breathlessly. 'I'll see you downstairs.'

It was going to be fine. Everything was in place and she was happy that it was. Her doubts had been banished, replaced with trust. Of course she would occasionally have doubts. This wasn't the future she had had in mind for herself, but Rocco had stepped up to the plate, proved himself worthy of her love, and she was determined to hang onto that.

The suite in which she now stood was lavish. She stepped into a small hall, adorned with an imposing tapestry on the wall, and from it she could see several doors opening out from a spacious living area to various rooms. The most eye-catching, however, was the bedroom, to which she quickly walked. She would like to have taken time to appreciate the splendour of the massive fireplace, the velvet drapes and the canopied bed with its sultry, deep-purple spread. A quick jump onto it wouldn't have gone amiss but, conscious of the time, she instead headed straight to the bathroom.

It was all marble. What else? There was a hot tub, deep bath, rainfall shower and, most impressive of all, floor-to-ceiling windows that overlooked the landscaped gardens at the back. Ella showered quickly. It took time to figure out the controls but she felt refreshed afterwards, although suddenly exhausted.

She dressed in one of the over-priced new outfits she had bought, a navy-blue cashmere dress that clung and showed off the beginnings of her bump in a way none of her baggy outfits did. She stared at her reflection in the long, freestanding mirror and was overwhelmed by a feeling of unreality.

Who was this person in a dress that cost more than her monthly salary, with shoes of the finest leather, staring out at manicured lawns that housed its own private chapel? And about to be married to a billionaire who had been brought up amidst this unbelievable grandeur.

She'd made a stand about continuing to work when the

baby was born but was that just a laughable notion? What was her life going to look like once she was married to Rocco? She was handing him her heart and putting all her trust in him. *Was that a wise decision?*

She felt the baby stir, a fluttering, butterfly feeling deep inside. She placed her hand on her tummy, took a deep breath and was relieved when a knock on the door told her that her escort had arrived—twenty minutes earlier than expected, so thank heavens she was ready and waiting. Make a late appearance and who knew? She didn't want to deal with thoughts that kept trying to surface, because there was no backing out now. But, with each deathly silent step towards whatever room Rocco was ensconced in with his parents, she could feel the drum beat of her heart getting louder with tension.

The door to a room on the ground floor was pushed open by the man who had led the way in silence. Ella blinked at the polished dark-wooden floor, the inlaid marble, the Persian rugs the original mouldings on the walls and the frescoed panels…all accented by the warm glow from the chandelier, with its fine crystal beads.

She noticed, with a flare of panic, that there was no sign of Rocco. Instead, there was just his parents, who both rose to their feet, which she could instantly see was a token gesture of welcome, because their faces were cold and unsmiling. They both had the same darkly striking beauty of their son but Ella's eyes were drawn to his mother, with her raven-black hair pulled back tightly into a chignon.

'Sit, please.'

'Where's Rocco?' Ella asked nervously.

'I have asked Rocco to deal with an urgent work-related issue but he will be here shortly. We thought we might get you here a little earlier so that we could acquaint ourselves with the woman who is suddenly to be our daughter-in-law.'

His father spread one arm towards an upright chair sandwiched between two long sofas and Ella obediently sat down and clasped her hands on her lap. She could have done with some water, because the glass would have given her something to fiddle with, but obviously whatever they wanted to say was more important than the ritual of offering drinks.

'We do not,' his mother said coldly, perching on the sofa to the left, while her husband mirrored her position on the opposite sofa, 'Have to tell you how shocked we both were when our son informed us that he was to be a father.'

'Naturally this was the last thing either of us expected.'

Sideswiped by what felt like a full-frontal attack without the courtesy of a preamble, Ella felt her body stiffen with tension. 'It was the last thing *I* expected, Señor and Señora Mancini. Believe it or not, my plans at this stage in my life didn't involve getting pregnant. But it's happened, and Rocco and I are both finding a way of dealing with it.'

'Our experience of women like you,' his mother said, 'Has been unfortunate, and you will excuse us if we are blunt on this matter.'

'Women like me?' Ella's head swivelled from left to right as she was besieged on both sides by the couple.

'Of course it is to be expected that our son would be targeted for his money. That has always been our fear.'

'I didn't *target* your son for his money! I didn't even know who Rocco was when I met him!' She looked at the door in desperation.

They were worried, she told herself, and that was to be expected. Yes, they came from stupid wealth; and yes, they would be on guard for people wanting to get a foot through the door so that they could get some of that money for themselves. They were naturally scared that she might be a gold-digger. It made perfect sense, really, when she thought about it. They didn't know just how much she loved their son, and they didn't know that he loved her as well, whether he could admit it or not. They were primed to be suspicious. Rocco had told her about his uncle. How else could they be expected to react to her except with suspicion and fear?

She took a few deep breaths to calm the rising tide of her anger. 'You don't have to fear that I'm after your son for his money,' she said coolly. She looked around at the lavish, funereal surroundings. 'I'm much more at home in simpler surroundings. I wouldn't dream of wanting any of this.'

'But this is where my son belongs,' his mother said with a stiff smile. 'You will be entering a great family house. You may say you are not interested in everything that comes with the Mancini name, but you will still have to do your duty as my son's wife, as you will likewise have to raise his heir to be the man who carries on the family name. I trust that all pre-nuptial agreements are signed and in order?'

'I think it's best if we move on from this, Señor and Señora Mancini. I can't say any more than I already have.

You'll just have to trust that I'm not out to fleece your son and I haven't contrived to get pregnant so that I could pin him down.'

'In which case, arrangements for the wedding will have to be discussed.'

Rocco's father finally stood to offer her something to drink and rang a bell to summon one of their staff when she opted for a glass of water.

'I realise you've only just found out… You probably haven't had time to think of anything…er…' Ella stumbled over her words while wondering whether Rocco intended to show up any time soon. Having said she could rely on him to be a protective wall between his parents and her, he had instead thrown her to the wolves and left her to fend for herself.

'I have already, naturally, been in touch with various people and given basic instructions on the sort of ceremony we have in mind.'

'You have?'

'This will be an illustrious event. Naturally, the sooner plans are put in motion, the better. What we cannot change, we must unfortunately accept. Rocco told us a week or so ago that he would be marrying. It does not afford us much time with a baby on the way so I have already begun to put things in place. At the very least, I have made a list of attendees. I would calculate that in the region of *quinientos invitados*…five hundred guests…'

'You've made a list…?'

The ground seemed to be opening up under her feet as she did the maths. His mother had known that they would be getting married a week ago? That was when Rocco had shown up out of the blue, when she had first broken the news to him. Yet he'd given her the impression that he had only just told his parents, as they were packing their bags to leave for Spain. Which meant...

Solid ground began to turn to quicksand and she licked her lips while her mind went blank, fighting against the very obvious conclusion that she had been deceived by Rocco yet again. She'd thought that he'd taken his time to win her over, to prove to her that he could be the man she wanted, even if he wasn't in love with her. That, whatever the outcome, he would respect her decision.

But he hadn't, had he? He'd gone right ahead and assumed that she would marry him, and had been so confident that he would get exactly what he wanted that he'd briefed his parents from the start. Had all that thoughtful, caring stuff just been an act to get her where he wanted her?

She felt sick at the thought of it, at the thought that she'd let stupid feelings, disingenuous love, hope and optimism get in the way of the common sense that had guided her at the very start.

There was no way on earth she would marry him now. She spun away and muttered that she was suddenly feeling queasy. Maybe the trip over...stress...perhaps she hadn't eaten enough...a ragtag jumble of nonsense... She left eyes down, not wanting to see those cold, disapproving faces for a second longer.

Tears blurred her eyes and every muscle in her body was rigid with tension as she moved stiffly towards the door, that was pulled open before she could get to it. And there he was, taking a few seconds to register that something was wrong, then glancing behind her to his parents before returning his dark gaze to her stricken face.

'What the hell is going on here?'

CHAPTER TEN

'I ASKED WHAT'S going on.'

The atmosphere was electric with tension. Instinct told Rocco that Ella was desperate to leave the room but he stayed her with one hand because he wanted to find out what the hell had just happened. No one was going to run away until he found out, and that included his parents, who had risen to their feet and were looking at him with thin lipped defiance.

His parents were punctual to the point of pathological. His father had dispatched him to check over something with one of the subsidiary companies, but he had made sure to head straight to the sitting room so that she didn't end up facing his parents without his reassuring presence.

He ushered Ella back into the room and dismissed the man who had appeared with a jug of water and a glass.

'What have you said to Ella?' He addressed his mother but included his father in his grim, unsmiling, narrow-eyed stare.

'We simply made it clear, Rocco, that we are not people to be taken in by anyone entering this family who might wish us harm.'

'You accused *my wife to be* of what, exactly? Of being a *gold-digger*?'

'We have enough experience of those sorts to be on guard.'

'Those sorts?' Rocco left that derogatory judgement simmering in the air between them for a few seconds.

'Is this all that was said?' He turned to Ella and felt something pierce deep inside him at the hurt and dismay on her pretty face. A surge of possessiveness, a driving urge to protect her, washed through him and he dimly recognised that it had nothing to do with the fact that she was carrying his child. He didn't need her to answer because he could take a pretty good shot at guessing just what had happened.

'You sent me off on a wild goose chase about something and nothing so that you could corner my fiancée and cause her distress?' he asked coldly.

His parents had the grace to flush and exchanged a quick look.

'We thought, Rocco, that…'

'I don't want to hear any of your excuses. You've upset Ella and, in my books, that is unforgivable. Let me make one thing absolutely straight.' He took a step towards his parents and outstared them. 'If you want anything to do with our child, then you will never say anything to Ella again that might upset her. Do I make myself clear?'

'There are duties that must be fulfilled. This is how you were raised, Rocco.'

'And rest assured what has to be done will always be done. In my way and on my terms. Now, I'm going to head upstairs with Ella and, when we return for dinner, no more will be said on this matter. I expect my fiancée to be treated as a welcome member of the Mancini family.'

Fine words, Ella thought. Yes, they'd warmed to her. It was nice that he'd stuck up for her, because she had been lost and out of her depth in the face of his icily disapproving parents. But no amount of warm sentiments could erase the bitterness of knowing that, in his mind, marrying her had been a fait accompli the second he'd known about the pregnancy.

Ella waited until they were in the bedroom before she turned to him, schooling her expression. How could he stand there, so beautiful, so sophisticated, so unfairly sexy, so ready to say what he knew she'd want to hear and knowing just how to deliver the words to the best possible effect?

'Thank you for having my back in there, Rocco.'

'I apologise for my parents. I'm afraid, this is who they are. I had, however, expected better from them. At the very least, a show of polite good will. It seems they dispatched me so that they could see you on your own and… well…again, I apologise on their behalf.'

'I understand their concerns. Maybe they thought you'd inherited your uncle's predisposition for ending up with someone out for his money.'

'You're upset. I get that. Do you want to skip the dinner they've had prepared? It might be better to face them, and I can assure you there won't be a repeat of what happened down there. You have my word.'

'Your word. Now, *that's* interesting, isn't it, Rocco?' Her words were cool and precise but her body still yearned for him in a way that made her feel angry, distraught and hopeless.

'What are you talking about?'

'You lied to me, didn't you?'

'I lied to you?' He stilled as wariness replaced the warm reassurances of moments ago.

'You made your mind up that we were going to get married from the very second I told you I was pregnant.' The heat coming from him was too much. He was too close to her. She couldn't think straight when she could breathe him in the way she could now. She watched in alarmed fascination as he strolled towards the window. He looked out for a couple of seconds then turned to look at her. She absolutely loathed the shudder of sexual awareness that rippled through her, alive and alert, despite the emotions raging through her.

'Ella, please...' He nodded to the velvet sofa by the window. 'Sit down and let's talk about this. You're pregnant. Getting stressed the way you are now isn't good for your blood pressure. You've already been stressed out enough by my parents.'

Ella stared at him expressionlessly for a few seconds and then heeded his advice, because her legs were wobbly, and she knew that he was right insofar as stress on her body wasn't a good idea.

'You were never going to take *no* for an answer, were you?' she said quietly. 'When I told you that I was pregnant, when you proposed marriage, I wasn't in favour of it. It was never where I saw my life going. It was never what I wanted. I wanted to be loved, to love someone, to know that there would be a strong bond between me and the father of my child—a bond glued together with all the love that came when two people *wanted* to spend their lives together. Not when two people felt they had no choice *but* to spend their lives together.

'You didn't love me, Rocco, and you were never going to love me. Not in the way you knew I wanted. But you didn't want an illegitimate child.' She looked around at the grand bedroom, the decades and decades of family wealth wrapped up in suffocating, restrictive traditionalism.

He was conditioned for this extraordinarily high level of obligation and duty. Maybe there had been that window of letting his hair down when they had first met, but he'd always known that that window was going to close. She understood him, and yet could never forgive what she now saw as a calculating attempt to win her over by pretending to be someone he wasn't.

'I can't deny that the thought of sharing custody of my own flesh and blood was abhorrent to me, Ella,' he admitted.

'Was it all a game for you?'

'What do you mean?'

'The way you set about proving to me that you could be the perfect father and the perfect husband. The way you strung me along, wearing me down a little at a time, having already spoken to your parents as though everything was a done deal.'

'You think I was acting out some part?'

'Haven't you done that before?' she asked tersely 'You were a certain *Jose Rivero* when we met, or have you forgotten that?'

'I thought we'd put that one to rest. Ella, I'll admit that

I wasn't going to give up on the notion of marrying you so that our child could get the very best life had to offer. And I don't mean all of this—' he waved a hand at their surroundings '—although *all of this* is substantial. I mean I was, and remain, convinced that becoming husband and wife is the right thing to do and always will be. Whether I informed my parents that this would be the case earlier than you thought doesn't change that fact.'

'It does for me.'

'What are you trying to say?'

'I want out. I can't go through with this.'

'What...?'

Ella steeled herself against the urgency in his voice which struck to the very core of her. Should she tell him honestly how she felt? Yes, she would do that and take the consequences. There had already been far too much deceit, concealment and dishonesty.

'It took a lot for me to trust you, Rocco. I was devastated when I discovered that you had lied to me about who you really were and I was even more shocked when you turned up out of the blue and admitted that you were the guy who was going to buy the department store.'

'I know that. You've already told me that.'

She swept past his interruption, 'I understood the reasoning behind the takeover, of course I did, but you still lied to me and it still left a sour taste in my mouth.'

'I had no choice. I thought we'd gone over all this.'

'Well, here we are, going over it again. After you showed back up, after you took the pregnancy so well, after you set out to prove to me that you were marriageable material even if marrying for the sake of a child had never been my life's ambition… Well, Rocco, I really began to believe you. More than that.'

'Yes?'

'I began to hope that what you felt might be more than just a sense of duty and obligation.' Hope, optimism and time would give her the outcome she'd wanted… How naïve she'd been.

'Love, Ella—it's not in my repertoire. I never led you to believe that it was. Did I?'

'No. No, I can see now that it was just me reading all sorts of stuff into some of the things you said and the confidences you shared with me.'

'Of course we shared things, Ella,' he said roughly, raking his fingers through his hair. 'It would have been unnatural, given the circumstances, if we hadn't.'

Ella could sense his discomfort. How tempting it would be to pull herself away from the brink. She knew that if she mumbled something, *anything*, about hormones, exhaustion or not being quite herself, if she laughed this earnest conversation off, he would happily sweep it all under the carpet and continue as though nothing had changed. He would be able to do that because on an emotional level he wasn't involved.

'Rocco, I didn't want to, but I fell in love with you. And I hoped that, in time, you would see that you'd fallen in love with me as well. But that's not going to happen. I thought you had emotions that were just never there. You knew you were going to marry me, you knew that was what you wanted, and nothing was going to get in the way of that. You did what it took but I can't marry a guy like you. I can't marry you and have my heart broken over and over again, every single day, because I would never stop wanting more than you could ever give me.'

She took a deep breath. 'Could you do that, Rocco? Give me what I want?'

Rocco felt the world come to a grinding halt.

In his fiercely controlled life, there was no room for the heady romanticism of love, and he had always projected the sort of demeanour that repelled women from going there. When the time came, he would take a wife, and it would be a sensible arrangement.

Hadn't he made it clear from day one that love with all its complications wasn't for him? She could hardly say that he had encouraged her to think that he would suddenly, against everything in his nature, fall in love with her. Hand over all his self-control into the safekeeping of someone else.

Because that was what love entailed, wasn't it? Yes, the pregnancy had generated a marriage proposal, and it was a proposal that made perfect sense. She, herself, had come round to that conclusion so why was she now braking to a halt because of the small issue of timing? The enormity of her decision rammed into him with brutal force.

'You want me to promise you something you know I can't do?' He thought of her walking away from him with wrenching pain. This was about the child they shared. He felt dizzy and panicked. All of this, simply because he had happened to tell his parents about the pregnancy and had naturally assured them that they would marry. He hadn't thought twice. He'd been confident because that was just the way he was.

And now… It was all slipping away but the thought of promising love, of her asking that of him…

'I thought you'd say that. It's going to be very difficult for me to remain here with this happening, Rocco.'

'I can't believe this.'

'I wanted to be completely honest with you, Rocco. I love you and you…you broke my heart, not once but twice. But I'll get over it because I know I deserve more than a man who breaks hearts. Nothing will change when it comes to the baby.'

Rocco looked at her. Was it his imagination or could he already see the shutters coming down? Her soul was turning to ice, sealing him off, because that was what happened when love was turned on its head.

He gazed down when she reached across to cover his hand with hers.

'We can still sign the documents and I will never, ever get in the way of you having access to your own flesh and blood. And, yes, I can see that this legacy belongs to your offspring.'

'Yes.'

'I realise that one day you'll meet someone, and I will as well, because we both deserve that. I'll meet someone who loves me, who would never lie to me, who appreciates me for who I am, for all the right reasons. And you'll meet someone…who makes sense, I guess. And, when that happens, it'll be a bridge we'll just have to cross. In the meantime… I don't want to stay here a minute longer. You're a billionaire, Rocco. You can do anything with the click of a finger. Could you maybe take me away from here by clicking your fingers? I just want this whole thing to be over now.'

Ella gazed out at a landscape of softly falling snow. She was back at home. She had been for nearly a week, ever since she had fled Rocco's palatial mansion and ran away from the love she'd set her heart on which would never materialise.

She'd told him that she couldn't stay a minute longer and he'd arranged everything with the ease of a man who could dial two numbers and get whatever he wanted. He'd begged her to stay the night—it was late and she would be mentally and physically exhausted. He would ensure she left first thing in the morning, unnoticed and without the trauma of having to socialise with his parents. He would explain the situation to them. They would accept it because they would have no choice. Just as she had left him with none.

Every single decent word that had passed his beautiful mouth had reminded her of all the foolish reasons she had seen more in their relationship than really existed. He didn't love her. He was just a fair-minded, honourable guy who would never give his heart to her, or maybe never *could*. What he had seen as a foregone conclusion—about which he had made assumptions about a future in which the concept of her not marrying him had never crossed his radar—she had seen as betrayal. And those were fundamental differences between them that could never be breached.

The reach of his privilege, of growing up with such immense wealth, had made him imperious, and it didn't matter whether he was honourable or not. He would always presume that his way was the best. He would, and never could, be the vulnerable man who would be able to meet her halfway.

Maybe he could only really fall in love with someone from his own class. She'd met his parents and it was easy to understand that he'd been raised to accept a certain type of woman as the ideal match. Nothing else was ever really going to do. He said he didn't believe in love but he probably just hadn't met the right woman who ticked all the boxes. When it came to anything emotional, Rocco would always view the world in black and white. But life wasn't black and white; the time would come when he would find that out but not with her.

Having a baby ticked an important box for him but he would come to thank her for walking away because, just as for her, all those other boxes also needed to be ticked beyond the one that came under the heading of 'duty'.

A driver had whisked her away from his family palace before half-past eight the following morning, and she had avoided seeing his parents, so had been spared any follow-up accusations.

And since then...

Her poor dad, silent, awkward and bursting with love and sympathy, had had to deal with her long face and bouts of tears. He handed her tissues and patted her on the back, trying hard to find the right words to comfort her, but there was part of her that was inconsolable.

Now, he was in the kitchen cooking dinner for them. She gazed around her at the wonderful, warm Christmas scene that had been filled with such hope and joy when, little more than two weeks ago, she and Rocco together had put up the Christmas tree and hung all the decorations.

Since she'd returned, she'd done her best to banish negative thoughts by going all out on the decorations, reminding herself that there was a lot to be grateful for, not least the little baby growing and kicking, having fun inside her. Above the stone fireplace, with its roaring fire keeping the winter cold at bay, evergreen garlands were threaded with red berries and pinecones, which she herself had fetched from the garden. She had hung the stocking she'd had since she'd been a kid and a new one for the baby inside her, which she would fill with little soft play treats.

Outside the snow was falling, as it had done for the past three days, lightly but persistently, blanketing the countryside and turning everything magical. She had put Christmas carols on the CD player her dad insisted on keeping, even though she'd tried to introduce him to some more advanced technology for listening to music. He'd had none of it. The background music was soothing and, staring out through the windows, stretched out on the large, comfy sofa with a soft throw over her, she almost felt at peace.

The sharp bang on the front door made her jolt upright.

'Dad?' she called out. 'Are you expecting anyone?'

Her dad bustled out of the kitchen, apron still round his waist, and looked between her and the door. 'Not in this weather, and not on Christmas Eve, love. Don't budge. I'll get the door.'

'Don't be silly.' Ella smiled at him and stifled a yawn.

It wasn't yet seven in the evening, but she could have slept for England. 'It's much more important for you to make sure the cooking gets done and all the prep for tomorrow. This pregnant lady needs to be spoiled, and I'm just quoting you on that. I'll get it.'

She slipped off the sofa, pleased to see her dad grin, a happy sort of 'my girl's back' grin. She pulled open the door, because in this part of the world that was what people did, and there he was—the guy whose image had haunted her every waking moment and most of the sleeping ones.

Ella was so shocked that for a few seconds she couldn't breathe. Yes, he'd contacted her, made sure she was okay. Just the dark timbre of his voice down the end of the phone had made her grit her teeth in frustration because he'd sounded so *normal*, while she was breaking up inside. He'd steered clear of conversation that might release any more emotional outpourings. One lot had clearly been quite enough, thank you very much. So she'd been left nursing her broken heart, not quite knowing what to do with it.

He'd set up an account for her and had transferred so much money that she'd protested.

'A house,' he'd said without bothering to allow her a protest vote. 'A car, living expenses... Accept it, Ella. There will be a lot more where that came from.'

He'd transferred her enough money to buy whatever house she wanted and the sort of ridiculously high-end car he was accustomed to owning. What had been the point of being coy?

She hadn't asked him how his parents had taken the

marriage being called off. She'd taken her cue from him and not mentioned anything at all that wasn't purely practical. It had been agony. He'd been so...*nice*. The nicer he'd been, the more she'd wanted him to show *something*. Anything.

Now, he stood in front of her in all his glory, and she couldn't manage to get a word out. The snow was settling on his dark, woollen coat and patent leather shoes. He had his hands shoved in his pockets as he stared at her. She felt a whoosh of pure love because she could recall every line and groove in his beautiful face.

'What are you doing here?'

'I've come to see you.'

This was right, coming here, stifling doubts that had been bred over a lifetime, doubts about trusting instinct and emotion and not being scared of them. Rocco sucked in a deep breath and stared at her. Even after she'd gone, he still hadn't quite believed it. He would have blamed his parents, but that would have been the easy way out, because he knew his parents for what they were. They were manacled to a belief system that he had always taken for granted, a belief system that might have worked for them but didn't work for him.

Had he ever thought for himself when it came to love and giving himself to someone else without restraint and with trust? No. Never. In every other area of his life, he had been high performing, brutally ambitious and fiercely proactive. But with his emotional life he had been lazy, and only when she'd walked away from him had he faced the truth about himself.

He'd met her and she had kick-started a process of self-discovery that had changed him. Maybe he'd just learned how to access what had always been there. She'd given him the chance to take off the clothes he had worn all his life, an outer shell wrapped up in duty, formality and the acceptance that throwing caution to the wind and loving someone utterly and completely wasn't for him.

He'd assumed that the lesson had been a two-week anomaly, but then she'd left him, and slowly he'd realised just how much he'd changed and just how much he'd found the way to love.

He needed to tell her all that but the green eyes inspecting him were narrowed and suspicious. As soon as he was in, and before he could divest himself of his coat, she stood back to the wall, her hands pressed together in front of her.

Ella knew that, however devastated she was by his rejection of her, she still had to communicate with him and accept the situation without bitterness or regret. She'd chosen to speak her mind and it wouldn't be fair to make him pay the price for not being on the same page as her.

Her father appeared in the doorway and Rocco turned round.

'Mind if I have a few words with your daughter, sir?'
'Nothing you couldn't say to her by post, young man?'
'No one uses the post any more, Dad.'

Ella couldn't manage to raise a smile when her father made a snort of disapproval under his breath but then he vanished back into the kitchen.

'If you need me to sign more stuff, then you could have let me know by email.'

'Can we sit down to have this conversation? Please?'

Rocco hesitated, for once not daring to presume that he wouldn't be thrown out by her.

'Why? What have you got to say? If it's not about practicalities, then it's because you want to try and convince me to marry you and to forget everything that went before.'

'I wouldn't do that, and that's not why I came.'

'You'd better come through and say your piece, Rocco. And I can tell you that the only reason I'm being hospitable is because we're going to be in one another's lives and we have to be able to communicate.'

'Understood.' He followed her into the sitting room and then looked around him at the familiar sight that had struck such a chord in him. 'Being here feels more like home than my own home did.'

'It's not going to work, Rocco. You can't just waltz in here and start playing more games to try and win me over.'

'The only thing I'm here to do is to ask you to listen to me. No game playing, Ella, not that I ever thought I played games with you.'

'What would you call "stringing me along"? Making me believe that you were Mr Perfect, when in fact you were just Mr Doing All He Can To Get Exactly What He Wants?'

'Will you listen to me? I won't be long but there are things I finally realise I need to say to you. Things I never thought about until I found I couldn't stop thinking about them.'

Ella stared at him narrowly. Her heart was still beating fast and her pulse was racing. She wanted him out of the house, and yet she couldn't bear the thought of him leaving now that he was here, because his presence fed her love and that feeling was consuming.

Plus she wanted to hear what he had to say. He looked tired and hesitant, two things she'd never associated with him. If this was going to be another ploy to get her back to the place she'd walked away from, then who wouldn't be curious to find out what his tactics were going to be?

But no tea or coffee. No getting comfy. No feet under the table. She didn't care how long it would have taken him to get here in poor weather.

'You have fifteen minutes,' she said flatly.

It was lovely and warm from the fire crackling in the stone hearth and the only light came from two table lamps and the standing lamp by the door. The air was scented by the Christmas tree, a fragrant pine smell that was all about the festive season. It made her think of when he'd last been here, when they'd decorated the tree together, when all her hopes had begun to bloom.

'When we met, Ella...that first time when you thought I was someone else... How do I explain this?' He leant forward, elbows resting on his thighs and his fingers clasped loosely together. 'I've spent the past week sifting through everything in my head, trying to work out how it was that I never realised...'

'Never realised *what*?' As her curiosity grew with dangerous speed, so did the sharpness of her voice, because she was determined to deny any more entries by him into her heart.

'That the man you made me feel like that first time—a man who was free and unweighted, and for the first time happy, really happy, in an unencumbered type of way—wasn't a flash in the pan because I was pretending to be someone else. That man was who I was always supposed to be. You unlocked the potential for joy inside me and left me wanting more.'

'Don't start spinning stories, Rocco. Is this just another twist on a ploy to get what you want? Does marriage and tradition mean that much to you?'

'That's what I'm saying now, Ella, my darling. Marriage and tradition count for nothing in the grand scheme of things.'

Darling... Ella shivered and clenched her fists in an effort to ward off the softening inside her at that term of endearment, spoken with such depth of feeling.

'I've lived my entire life so grounded in thinking that I knew exactly what I wanted from life that, when the unexpected came along in the form of you, I still carried on thinking that I could extinguish all the weird and wonderful things happening inside me. That I could explain it all away until...until I find that I can't.'

He looked around him. 'This is what I want and all I want—the peace and simplicity of what love brings because it doesn't have to be chaotic and ruinous. It doesn't have to be the emotional freefall of my uncle, or the acrimony of the divorced people I've met, or the stiff formality of my parents. Everyone's different and I want us to be the ones who succeed. I want us to be like your parents. I want to take the chance.'

'Rocco...'

'I know you don't want to believe a word I'm saying, because you think I've deceived you in the past, but

Ella... I'm asking you to marry me for all the right reasons. I'm asking you to marry me because I've fallen in love with you and because I can't see a life without you in it by my side. I want you and need you but... I get it.'

Their eyes tangled, and in that moment Ella knew that every word he spoke came from the heart. She had a euphoric surge of sheer joy as dreams she thought had been shattered now settled into place. Dreams she knew were going to come true.

'I love you, my darling, but know this—if you don't want to marry me, if it's too little, too late, then there will never be another woman for me. I will remain yours for ever.'

He reached into his pocket and, just like that, without ceremony—although she noted that his hand was shaking ever so slightly—he opened the small, black velvet box. Nestled inside was the most beautiful engagement ring she could have imagined. No adolescent daydream could ever have conjured up something so perfect—the round, flawless diamond took centre stage on the sleek, simple band of platinum.

'I'm offering this to you with love in my heart, Ella. Please, my darling, tell me that you'll be mine for ever.'

'Oh Rocco,' Ella breathed, finally allowing herself to feel all the love she had been so desperately trying to stifle. 'I want to marry you with all my heart...and for all the reasons you want to marry me.'

She watched him slip the ring on her finger and felt tears prick the back of her eyes. She looked at him, then glanced through the window at the steadily falling snow, then around the room where so many memories had been made of wonderful Christmases celebrated with family.

The door was opening to more Christmases spent with love and contentment as a family and, wherever they were, Ella knew that they would always be exactly the sort of Christmases she'd always dreamed of.

EPILOGUE

Ella had one last look at the Christmas tree in front of her, the tree she and Rocco had chosen and put up the week before. She closed her eyes and smiled, reliving the memory of them decorating it while baby Louisa Isabella had watched with lively interest from the baby bouncer, her pudgy legs kicking merrily away, mesmerised by the lights on the tree.

How could life possibly get more perfect? She was married to the man she adored, a guy who never tired of showing her just how much he adored her right back. They had married before their daughter was born, without fuss on a fine spring day. First in the church in the village where she had grown up, and then a blessing in a rather more formal ceremony in Madrid, a ceremony worthy of a Mancini. Like adversaries learning to circle one another, she and Rocco's parents had begun the journey towards communication without resentment.

The house they had chosen to live in was close enough to London for Rocco to comfortably commute but sufficiently far out for a garden big enough for fruit trees, a vegetable corner and enough space for all the equipment Rocco was looking forward to buying.

She heard her name being called and she hurried off to the kitchen where the smells of Christmas lunch made her stomach churn. She knew what she would find and she was already smiling at the thought of it.

And sure enough, as she entered the kitchen, there they all were—her beloved family. Rocco and her dad were busily cooking together, which was a terrific achievement, because his original plan had been to have the entire meal catered by a top chef and delivered in style to the house. He laughed when she'd shot that idea down in flames and had told her he hadn't thought for a minute that she'd agree.

Baby Louisa was sleeping peacefully through the chaos, her baby bouncer on the kitchen table. Ella thought she was probably worn out at having to witness her dad and granddad getting in each other's way in the kitchen although, it had to be said, the outcome looked excellent.

She and Rocco had invited his parents, but they had declined, although without rancour. Ella had thought she'd seen the older woman actually stifle a smile of resignation at the formal luncheon they would be obliged to host, as they had done for decades.

In three days, they would fly to Madrid and celebrate on a much smaller scale. The wedding had thawed them but it was the arrival of their granddaughter that had really done the trick and now, a year later... Yes, there was definite light at the end of the tunnel.

Throw another baby into the mix and who knew? BFFs

was her hopeful thought, not least because she could see how much Rocco's relationship with them was changing as they came to accept how much their son loved her.

Another baby...

Ella smiled and thought of the night that lay ahead and decided, *tonight looks like a good night to conceive...*

* * * * *

If you couldn't get enough of Heir for the Holidays, *then make sure to catch up on these other sparkling stories by Cathy Williams!*

Royally Promoted
Emergency Engagement
Snowbound Then Pregnant
Her Boss's Proposition
Billionaire's Reunion Bargain

Available now!

Get up to 4 Free Books!

We'll send you 2 free books from each series you try PLUS a free Mystery Gift.

FREE Value Over **$25**

Both the **Harlequin Presents** and **Harlequin Medical Romance** series feature exciting stories of passion and drama.

YES! Please send me 2 FREE novels from Harlequin Presents or Harlequin Medical Romance and my FREE gift (gift is worth about $10 retail). After receiving them, if I don't wish to receive any more books, I can return the shipping statement marked "cancel." If I don't cancel, I will receive 6 brand-new larger-print novels every month and be billed just $7.19 each in the U.S., or $7.99 each in Canada, or 4 brand-new Harlequin Medical Romance Larger-Print books every month and be billed just $7.19 each in the U.S. or $7.99 each in Canada, a savings of 20% off the cover price. It's quite a bargain! Shipping and handling is just 50¢ per book in the U.S. and $1.25 per book in Canada.* I understand that accepting the 2 free books and gift places me under no obligation to buy anything. I can always return a shipment and cancel at any time. The free books and gift are mine to keep no matter what I decide.

Choose one:
- ☐ **Harlequin Presents Larger-Print** (176/376 BPA G36Y)
- ☐ **Harlequin Medical Romance** (171/371 BPA G36Y)
- ☐ **Or Try Both!** (176/376 & 171/371 BPA G36Z)

Name (please print)

Address   Apt. #

City   State/Province   Zip/Postal Code

Email: Please check this box ☐ if you would like to receive newsletters and promotional emails from Harlequin Enterprises ULC and its affiliates. You can unsubscribe anytime.

Mail to the Harlequin Reader Service:
IN U.S.A.: P.O. Box 1341, Buffalo, NY 14240-8531
IN CANADA: P.O. Box 603, Fort Erie, Ontario L2A 5X3

Want to explore our other series or interested in ebooks? Visit www.ReaderService.com or call 1-800-873-8635.

---

*Terms and prices subject to change without notice. Prices do not include sales taxes, which will be charged (if applicable) based on your state or country of residence. Canadian residents will be charged applicable taxes. Offer not valid in Quebec. This offer is limited to one order per household. Books received may not be as shown. Not valid for current subscribers to the Harlequin Presents or Harlequin Medical Romance series. All orders subject to approval. Credit or debit balances in a customer's account(s) may be offset by any other outstanding balance owed by or to the customer. Please allow 4 to 6 weeks for delivery. Offer available while quantities last.

Your Privacy—Your information is being collected by Harlequin Enterprises ULC, operating as Harlequin Reader Service. For a complete summary of the information we collect, how we use this information and to whom it is disclosed, please visit our privacy notice located at https://corporate.harlequin.com/privacy-notice. Notice to California Residents – Under California law, you have specific rights to control and access your data. For more information on these rights and how to exercise them, visit https://corporate.harlequin.com/california-privacy. For additional information for residents of other U.S. states that provide their residents with certain rights with respect to personal data, visit https://corporate.harlequin.com/other-state-residents-privacy-rights/.